“I don’t think s

at me tonight w

I don’t think you do, either.” She had that right, but the chances of the shooter staying behind after they’d hightailed it out of there were slim.

“I know things—” she laced her fingers together and set her elbows against her knees “—didn’t end well... But I’m hoping we can move past this awkwardness—or whatever it is—between us. I can only imagine how much you hate me for leaving, but I appreciate your help.” A half smile pulled at one corner of her mouth. “Truce?”

“I don’t hate you, Glennon. Trust me, I’ve tried.” The words were out of his mouth before he had a chance to think about their meaning. But it was the truth.

RULES IN
RESCUE

NICHOLE SEVERN

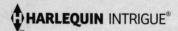

For my readers.

I finished this book a month before I gave birth to my second demon spawn.

It was nice knowing you while I was still sane.

ISBN-13: 978-1-335-60419-4

Rules in Rescue

Copyright © 2019 by Natascha Jaffa

Recycling programs
for this product may
not exist in your area.

This edition published by arrangement with Harlequin Books S.A.

For questions and comments about the quality of this book, please contact us at CustomerService@Harlequin.com.

Printed in U.S.A.

Nichole Severn writes explosive romantic suspense with strong heroines, heroes who dare challenge them and a hell of a lot of guns. She resides with her very supportive and patient husband, as well as her demon spawn, in Utah. When she's not writing, she's constantly injuring herself running, rock climbing, practicing yoga and snowboarding. She loves hearing from readers through her website, www.nicholesevern.com, and on Twitter, @nicholesevern.

Books by Nichole Severn

Harlequin Intrigue

Rules in Blackmail
Rules in Rescue

Visit the Author Profile page at Harlequin.com.

CAST OF CHARACTERS

Anthony Harris—He can't refuse Glennon's plea to help recover her missing partner. He'll risk his life to keep her safe, but losing his heart to the woman who walked out on him is an entirely different matter.

Glennon Chase—When she starts investigating her partner's disappearance, there's only one man Glennon trusts to keep her alive—but Anthony's refusal to help means she'll have to reveal a truth about their past not even the military has uncovered.

Bennett Spencer—After sending Glennon a mysterious message, the CID special agent has disappeared. The closer Anthony and Glennon get to recovering her missing partner, the more they're convinced Bennett isn't what he seems.

Nicholas Mascaro—Suspected of orchestrating the sale of millions of dollars of military weapons stolen from bases all around the country, Sergeant Mascaro has been court-martialed and sentenced for his crimes. But it looks like someone has taken his place at the head of the operation, and they'll do anything to keep Glennon from discovering the truth.

Elizabeth Dawson—As a former consultant for the NSA, Elizabeth is capable of building or destroying lives with the touch of a button, but uncovering who wants Glennon dead may be one of her toughest challenges yet.

Chapter One

"I need your help," she said.

Four simple words had ripped weapons expert Anthony Harris away from his current surveillance assignment and into downtown Anchorage at three in the morning.

And there she was. Glennon Chase—his ex-fiancée—needed him after all this time.

"I haven't heard from you in almost five years and now you need my help?" The weight of the Beretta M9 in his shoulder holster kept him focused on the situation at hand and not on the shadows under those hazel-specked green eyes. He shouldn't have come. Too much history between them. Too easy to get wrapped up in her again. "Don't you have an entire team of soldiers to help you with whatever investigation you're working?"

The muted beam from her flashlight streaked across the pitted hardwood floors of the abandoned house. She'd given him the address over the phone, insisted he couldn't be followed. Because she wasn't supposed to be there. According to his contact, the Military Police Corps had assigned her to investigate the theft of a weapons shipment out of Joint Base Elmendorf Richardson. So why had Glennon told her superior officer she was on base when, in reality, she was about to be charged with breaking and entering downtown?

"I'm not here on an official investigation." Her gaze darted out the front window, her fingers visibly tightening around the flashlight. Nervous? That wasn't like her. At least, not the Glennon he knew. Correction: had known. A lot had changed over the last five years. Her dirty-blond hair, now darker than he remembered, had been pulled back in a loose ponytail. Nothing like the polished, professional way she used to wear it. Long, lean muscle peeked out from under her thin T-shirt, a far cry from the soft features he'd loved all those years ago. She'd always been strong, but she'd obviously been pushing herself physically since the last time they'd been in the same room together. And damn, she looked good.

"My partner, Bennett Spencer…he's missing. You're the only one who can help me find him," she said.

"A missing persons case." Tension flooded through the tendons along his shoulders, pulling his Kevlar vest tighter. Blackhawk Security's CEO, Sullivan Bishop, had hired him as a weapons expert, using his knowledge from over a decade with the 75th Ranger Regiment to the team's advantage. War, death, murder. He'd seen it all. But this…this was different. He'd been trained in recovery and rescue, but every cell in his body screamed he shouldn't have come. Partnering with his ex? Flat-out dangerous. "You need the police. Not me."

"The police can't help me." She took a single step toward him, hesitant. Desperation seeped into her movements, in the way she held so tightly onto the flashlight in one hand and her Glock in the other. Something had scared her—or someone. And while the idea she'd been rattled didn't sit well, this wasn't the assignment for him. The past had to stay in the past. He'd moved on. She had to do the same.

Her voice dipped into a whisper. "You're the only one I can trust."

He held back a laugh. Trust? That word meant nothing to her. Anthony shortened the distance between them, the hairs on the back of his neck rising. Heat simmered under his sternum. "What would you know about trust?"

Her brows drew inward, her one and only tell when things didn't go her way. Nice to see he could still get to her.

"I know what you must think of me, but I wouldn't have called unless I was absolutely sure about getting you involved. I can't do this alone," she said. "There's no one else who can help me. Please."

What the hell had she gotten herself into here? He scanned the rest of the street out the dirt-covered front window. The cul-de-sac looked like any other neighborhood downtown. Snow piled up in yards and on flat roofs, white brick with a few scattered trees clinging to the structures. The Kevlar weighed him down as he scanned the rest of their surroundings. No movement on the street, no shifting of shadows.

Taking a deep breath, he forced himself back into the moment. "Sorry. You've got the wrong guy. I'm sure the army can help you find the right one."

Anthony turned back the way he'd come. The dilapidated floorboards creaked under his steps.

"I have a son," she said.

Ice ran through his veins and he stopped cold. Heart thundering in his chest, he tried to wrap his head around her words. A son? He turned around slowly, the house protesting his shifting weight. He ran the numbers. They hadn't seen each other in five years, not since she'd walked out on him while he'd been on tour. A slight tremor shook his hand.

"How…" How old? He clenched his jaw. No. It wasn't possible. She wouldn't have left if she'd been pregnant. She would've told him. Which meant she had moved on. Just without him. "Why are you telling me this?"

"I'm going after my partner with or without your help." Moonlight crawled across her features as she moved toward him. The shadow along one side of her face shifted as she widened her stance. "My son has a better chance of his mother coming home if you have my back."

That was how she was going to play this? Putting the blame on him if something happened to her. As if blame hadn't already eaten him from the inside. He faced her completely, a hint of the rage he'd held back when she'd left bubbling to the surface. "You have some nerve—"

A laser sight crawled across Glennon's T-shirt.

Anthony lunged. The front window exploded as the echo of a single rifle shot rang through his ears. He crushed her into the floor then rolled them both near the wall. The world spun, but adrenaline kept him focused and alert as it had in far too many situations just like this. Single shooter armed with a sniper rifle. The echo of the shot died fast, but not before he'd pinpointed the shooter's location: the trees south of the house.

Anthony raised his head above the windowsill, his knees on either side of Glennon's waist, and scanned the tree line. The Beretta found its way into his hand. Wood exploded to his left as another bullet ripped through the darkness. He ducked below the window to avoid losing his head.

Glennon had clamped a hand over her left shoulder, both her gun and flashlight discarded on the floor where he'd tackled her. The small amount of moonlight reaching them showed something dark and wet spreading through her fingers. Blood. She'd been shot. Squinting, she let a small groan vibrate through her.

Peeling her hand back, Anthony scanned her shoulder. "Can you move?"

A scream escaped her control, singeing his nerve endings. She rolled onto her side and pushed herself upright. "I'm fine. Just get us out of here."

He aimed for the now motionless trees and fired. Three rounds. Four. The gun kicked back in his hand with each pull of the trigger. No movement. No return fire. The shooter had done what he'd come to do and disappeared. Or maybe not.

Hell. Pulse pounding hard in his throat, Anthony holstered his gun then reached for her. Wrapping one arm around her back and the other in her hand, he wrenched Glennon off the floor and into his side. Her roselike scent—a scent that seemed to cling to him—claimed his attention as they moved through the house. He couldn't focus on that now. There were no guarantees the shooter had vanished or that he'd come alone, but they weren't going to sit around and wait to find out.

Mentally alert. Physically strong. Morally straight, he reminded himself. The words had been drilled into his mind at boot camp.

Glennon picked up her discarded weapon. Moving when he moved, turning when he turned, she followed his lead, not missing a beat. "Do you want to help me now?"

Want to? Hell, no. Need to? Apparently.

"Do you really want to have this conversation while you're bleeding?" He steered them toward the north end of the house, opposite the shooter's last known position. If they had any chance of making it to his SUV without being shot, this was it. One hundred yards. That was all they had before they reached the vehicle, but that distance could feel like a mile when under fire. Pulling up short of the slashed screen door at the back of the house, Anthony scanned her from head to toe. "Ready?"

She nodded, blood coating her gun hand.

"Keep low, move fast and use me as cover if you have to." He didn't give her a chance to respond as he kicked the screen door aside and rushed them onto the covered back porch. A gust of freezing December air took the breath from his lungs. Hiking the Beretta shoulder-level, he sidestepped along the side of the house, making them as small a target as possible in case the shooter decided to come around the corner.

Snow crunched under their steps. Once they reached the corner of the house, they could make a run for it. Until then, the snow would only slow them down. Instincts on high alert, he listened for movement—anything—that pointed to an ambush.

"On my count." He had the SUV in his sights and Glennon glued to his side. "One." He studied the fast-spreading pattern of blood across her T-shirt. "Two." There were no other options at this point. They had to run. Now. He slowed his breathing, wrapped his free hand around her upper arm. A rush of electricity shot through him at the contact. "Three."

They raced toward the open white-picket-fence gate. A third shot exploded from the trees. Then a fourth. Anthony maneuvered Glennon to his opposite side, using his body as a shield, and emptied the Beretta's magazine toward the trees.

Alaska winters were some of the darkest on the planet. He couldn't see a damn thing, let alone narrow down the shooter's location in a patch of thick trees without stopping. Getting Glennon to safety had to be his priority. Pocketing the empty gun as they crossed the cul-de-sac, he unholstered another weapon and fired.

"Go, go, go!" Fifty feet. Thirty. The SUV came to life at the press of a button and, within seconds, he'd shoved Glennon into the back seat. He ripped open the driver's door, hiked himself behind the wheel and rammed the vehicle into Reverse. The houses that lined the street blurred as he leveraged his arm against the passenger's headrest and slammed his foot against the accelerator. One last bullet fought to penetrate the windshield as he maneuvered the SUV out of the neighborhood, tires screaming in protest, but didn't make it through. One of the perks of working for a heavily resourced security company: bulletproof glass. He'd never been more grateful for it than right that second.

He spun the vehicle around and sped away from the abandoned house and the single shadowed figure standing in the middle of the street. The gunfire died, his fight-or-flight response returning to normal. The SUV's engine roared as he pushed it faster. One glance at Glennon in the rearview mirror and he white-knuckled the steering wheel. He inhaled deeply to slow his racing heart rate. "You still alive?"

"I'm alive. Thanks to you." She refused to look at him, staring out one of the back windows. Pretending the last few minutes hadn't happened—that she hadn't just been shot—wouldn't get her out of answering his questions.

He relaxed against the seat, finally able to take a full breath since setting foot in that house. "Good, then you can tell me who the hell tried to kill you."

SEVENTY-TWO HOURS. That was how long her partner, Sergeant Bennett Spencer, had been missing.

Criminal Investigations Special Agent Glennon Chase read his last text message on her phone's screen for the hundredth time as the SUV plowed through the snow-covered streets of her hometown.

I found proof.

What did it mean? She hadn't been able to locate him since. He wouldn't return her calls, hadn't been seen anywhere near his army barracks or shown up at the temporary office they'd been assigned to complete their investigation. On top of that, the GPS on his phone had gone offline. Or been destroyed.

But Bennett was alive. She had to believe that. Otherwise…

"Your guess is as good as mine at this point." Glennon pressed her palm against the bullet wound in her left shoulder as she shifted in the back seat. Pain flooded through her but it kept her focused. In the moment. Her attention slid to the wall of pure muscle in the driver's seat. Because letting her guard down around Sergeant Major Anthony Harris would be a mistake she couldn't afford. Not again.

The former Ranger hadn't changed a bit. Aviator sunglasses hanging from his T-shirt, sandy-brown hair, full beard, thick muscles strapped inside that familiar Kevlar vest adorned with a patch of the Grim Reaper. Gun at his side. He was attractive, intelligent, protective—everything she'd imagined she'd needed when they'd first gotten together after basic training. He'd still been in the army then, her weapons instructor out of Fort Benning. And those eyes… the darkest blue she'd ever encountered. Dark and deadly.

"Hope a bullet in the shoulder was worth it." Anthony kept his focus on the road, but the dangerous sinking of his tone meant his focus rested one hundred percent on what had happened back at that house. She didn't blame him. An ambush had been the last thing on her mind when she'd tracked Bennett's GPS to that location. "Did you at least find what you were looking for?"

Right. Focus. She swallowed the rush of warmth spreading through her chest and stared out the passenger-side window into the cold. "You mean aside from proof someone doesn't want me to find my partner?" She inhaled through another round of pain and pressed her shoulders into the leather seat as a distraction. "No."

The house had been abandoned long before she'd gotten there, but Bennett's GPS hadn't lied. He'd been there for close to an entire day before his phone had been turned off. Or died. Which didn't make sense. They'd been assigned by the provost marshal general to investigate a stolen shipment of military hardware out of JBER here in Anchorage. Guns, ammunition, rocket launchers. At no point in their investigation had an abandoned house located downtown come into the equation. Bennett shouldn't have been there.

"One-word answers aren't going to help me keep you alive." The rough edge to Anthony's voice added to the weight in her stomach.

Relief flooded through her, however fleeting. She shouldn't have called him, but after two days of no leads and running into dead ends, she'd run out of options. Going to the police, even involving the army in her partner's disappearance, could put her son in danger. Because while she didn't know exactly what'd happened to Bennett, her gut said he hadn't walked away. In the end, Anthony was the only person she could trust not to get himself killed and to protect her in the process. "Does that mean you've decided to help me?"

Anthony pressed a button hidden beneath the driver's sun visor and swung the SUV down into an underground parking garage. The building wasn't familiar. At least, she didn't recognize it. Several SUVs, exactly like his, lined the parking stalls. No other personnel were visible in the cement fortress. No security guards. No employees. The place was empty.

"We're here," he said.

She caught sight of four cameras mounted to the ceiling, all with small red lights beneath the lenses. That, coupled with the Batcave entrance, gave her an idea of where they'd ended up.

Blackhawk Security. His new employer.

Anthony shouldered his way out of the vehicle and rounded back to open her door for her, weapon in hand. Always the gentleman, always prepared for the worst.

"I've got to say, I never imagined you working in the private sector." He certainly hadn't been willing to change careers when they'd been a couple.

She slid out of the SUV, but fell into him when another round of pain shot across her shoulder. With one hand on his chest to keep from face-planting on the cement, she tried to ignore the seductive heat snaking through her. Being shot at, taking a bullet—that she could handle. It'd been part of her job since the day she'd been promoted to special agent within CID. But being this close to him, his clean, masculine scent resurrecting countless nights spent wrapped in each other's arms... Glennon added another foot of space between them.

No. Despite her need for Anthony's help, that was as far as it'd go between them. Nothing more. She pulled away. Her voice wavered as she forced her gaze from his. Or was it from the blood loss? "What finally made you decide to leave the wars behind?"

"We need to take a look at that wound." He slammed the door closed behind her and headed for the single elevator on the north side of the parking garage. Studying their surroundings, he adjusted his vest. Ready for anything.

A rush of warmth crawled into her neck and face as she kept on his heels. The elevator doors closed behind them, her stomach dropping as they ascended to the top floor. Whether it was from the change in elevation or being caged in a small container with the one man she thought she'd never see again, she didn't know. Didn't matter. She had a job to do and the bullet tearing through her left shoulder should've kept reminding her of that.

With a muted ding, the elevator doors parted

and they stepped onto a darkened floor. It was after hours. Most Blackhawk Security personnel had obviously gone home for the day, but Anthony led her to a single lit room at the end of the hall.

A breathtaking view of the Chugach Mountain range took up the entire east side of the floor, and her insides ached. This had been her home for most of her life. She'd loved it. The wildlife, the snow, the sunsets and beautiful lakes. Leaving this city—she glanced at Anthony—leaving *him* had been one of the hardest decisions she'd ever made. Even if it had been the only option at the time.

"I've already called in the rest of the team." Anthony diverted her to a hallway to his left, bypassing an occupied conference room, and motioned her inside the first door. "But I'm going to check out that wound first."

"Like I said back at the scene, I'm fine." She'd taken a bullet before. And lived. But he didn't need to know the details of that particular investigation. "I came to you to keep me alive, and so far, you've done a bang-up job. Now, let me do mine."

She made her way back to their original route and swung the floor-to-ceiling oak door open with her uninjured arm. The large conference room was dominated by men and women she assumed made up the founding core of Blackhawk Security. One stood immediately, striding toward her with his hand extended. He was muscular, although not quite as big as Anthony. Dark hair and a five-o'clock shadow were eclipsed by his sharp sea-blue eyes. "Sullivan Bishop, CEO of Blackhawk Security. You must be Ms. Chase. We've heard a lot about you."

"Sergeant Chase." Probably nothing good, considering how things had ended between her and Anthony. She wrapped her blood-free hand around Sullivan's calloused grip. "But as much as I love the chitchat, I don't have a lot time. My partner is missing and the longer I'm here, the less likely I'll find him alive. So I need Anthony to help in the recovery. I'll pay whatever fee you set. There's just one condition—you can't involve the authorities or the army."

"All right. Then let's get to the point, Sergeant." Sullivan threw Anthony an amused smile before dropping her hand and folding his arms across his chest. His stance screamed military—wide legs, impossible to push over if she tried. A SEAL, if she had to guess. She could tell by the haircut. "Who put that bullet in your shoulder and why?"

Anthony threaded his fingers around her uninjured arm, hiking her into his side. "She needs to get this wound checked before we get into this."

Hadn't they already covered this?

"I have no idea." Stinging pain worked through her as she wrenched out of his hold to take a seat. As much as she appreciated his concern, they didn't have time for this. Flashes of the night's events were fresh in her mind and she needed to remember every detail. Talking it through was the only way to do that. The shooter could be anywhere by now.

Collapsing back into one of the leather chairs, she exhaled hard, checking her wound. No major damage. She'd live, but she'd need a good cleaning, and stitches front and back. "But I'm positive it has to do with my partner's disappearance. I tracked Sergeant Spencer's phone GPS to that location. Obviously someone doesn't want me following in his footsteps."

Anthony took a seat two chairs down, her awareness of him at an all-time high.

"Could it have been your partner who pulled that trigger?" Another member of the team leaned forward in his chair, fingers laced on the dark reflective wood. His expression seemed to light up at the idea.

She'd done research on the people in this room before dialing Anthony's number. Sullivan Bishop: CEO. Elizabeth Dawson: network security. Kate Monroe: profiler. Vincent Kalani: forensics. She'd had to know what kind of support—if any—she'd have access to during her off-the-books investigation. But something about Elliot Dunham, Blackhawk Security's con-artist-turned-private-investigator, made her hope the firm had a whole lot of hazard insurance to keep him on their payroll. "It's not him. I know Bennett. He'd never take a shot at me."

"It's amazing what some people will do to keep

their secrets safe." Elliot smiled. "And going to the police is a bad idea because…?"

All eyes landed on her, a physical pressure holding Glennon in her chair. "The fewer people involved, the better."

She had her own secrets. Granted they wouldn't stay buried forever, but she wasn't about to reveal them right here, right now. And not to these people. She glanced toward her ex-fiancé, every muscle in her body strung tight. A rush of dizziness crashed through her and she checked her stained shirt. Too much blood loss. Damn it. Maybe she should've listened to him after all. She couldn't go on like this much longer.

Gripping the table hard, Glennon tried to breathe through the darkness closing around the edges of her vision. "On second thought, I think I'll take you up on that patch job now."

Chapter Two

Memories could only get a man so far.

Having Glennon here, his hands on her skin, resurrected those irrational feelings he thought he'd buried a long time ago. He wiped the excess blood from her wound, doing everything in his power not to crowd her as he worked. That was the thing about Glennon. She urged him to get closer, pulling him in with her scent, the brightness in her gaze and her smile. But she'd made herself perfectly clear when she'd tugged her arm out of his hold in the conference room. Calling him tonight had been strictly business.

"How bad is it?" A hiss escaped from between her teeth as he inspected the wound for shrapnel, but she turned her head away to hide her reaction. Exhaustion wreaked havoc under her eyes, but she wouldn't admit she needed sleep. Wouldn't admit she needed anything. Always insisted on taking care of herself. Which made her asking for his help in the middle of the night…suspicious.

"Could've been worse. Looks like a through-and-through. Just the one piece of shrapnel." He'd seen plenty of bullet wounds on tour. Not for the faint of heart, but she held her own.

Anthony discarded the sliver of metal and bloody gauze into the biohazard bin then reached for the needle and thread he'd already prepped. Crude, but she'd asked for a fast patch job. No anesthetic. No doctor consult.

"Good." Glennon tugged at her T-shirt and sports bra to give him better access. All that perfect, creamy skin exposed only for him. "Let's get this over with."

Pinching the wound with sanitized hands, he sutured the sides closed. The rise and fall of her lean shoulders set his heart rate at an easy rhythm. As much as he'd wanted to hunt down that shooter on his own to make the bastard pay for putting a bullet in her, relief spread through him. She was alive. That was all that mattered. She'd asked him to protect her, and he'd done his job. But pulling bullet fragments from her shoulder wouldn't be the end of it. Not in the least.

Silence descended in a physical pressure against his chest. He'd imagined this day, the one where he'd be face-to-face with her again. He'd demand a reason for her leaving, try to explain why he'd gone on yet another tour. The conversations had played through his head on a near constant loop since the day he'd come home to the empty house they'd shared. But none of his fantasies had included a bullet in her shoulder or Glennon centered in a sniper's crosshairs. He swallowed back violent ideas of revenge sprinting through his head. He had to focus on something else. Anything else but her. "How old is your son?"

The idea she'd been with other men since leaving—had had a child with one of them—tightened the muscles down his spine. It shouldn't have. They hadn't been together in five years. So why did the thought of her moving on make him tighten his grip around the needle?

Her rough exhale cooled the overheated skin down his forearm. "I think it'd be better for both of us if we stick to talking about Bennett's disappearance, don't you?"

"All right." Anthony tied off the suture and used the scissors from the first-aid kit to clip it short. He taped a piece of gauze over her wound to keep the stitches dry then disinfected and packed up the medical supplies. The patch job disappeared as she maneuvered her clothing back into place.

Focus on her missing partner? No problem. Compartmentalization had become one of his best skills. He exhaled to rid his system of her intoxicating scent, the one that kept pulling him in closer. "Our forensics guy, Vincent, pulled the bullet from the windshield of the SUV, but we won't know where it came from for a few more hours. You can grab a change of clothes from Elizabeth and crash in one of the empty offices until then."

"No." Glennon shook her head as she hiked her jacket over her shoulder, wincing. "I'll take the change of clothes, but I'm going back to that house as soon as possible."

He faced her. Go *back*? Was she insane? Before he knew it, he was in front of her, forcing her to look up at him. An icy feeling crashed through him. He'd almost lost her back at that house. Now she wanted to put her life in danger a second time in less than two hours? His six-foot-four-inch frame towered over her but Glennon held her ground. "Because one bullet wound wasn't enough? Are you going for a shot in the head this time?"

"I came here to find my partner and that's exactly what I'm going to do," she said. "Sergeant Spencer's GPS put him in that house for over twenty-four hours. And since I didn't have a chance to search the place properly before someone tried to shoot me, I'm going back. You can either come with me to make sure it doesn't happen again or give me a set of car keys. Your choice."

"You could've died back there, Glennon." Right in front of him, no less. And that wasn't an option. He'd seen enough death in combat to last him two lifetimes. He wasn't going for three. Her natural warmth worked through his T-shirt, raising his awareness of how close he'd gotten to her. Or maybe it was the flat-out fear of her taking another bullet that put him on edge. "You're not stepping out of this building without protection."

"Good. Then we have a deal. Now let's get to work." She stepped away from him, slowly this time, but the pressure in his lungs refused to let up. That seemed to happen a lot since she'd come back into his life a few hours ago.

Despite the size of the medical suite, Glennon took her original seat beside him. She extracted her phone from her jacket pocket and handed it to him. "Bennett sent me a message right before he disappeared."

"'I found proof.'" Anthony noted the edge of the photo behind the message, a boy with buzzed blond hair and the hint of a wide smile, but nothing more. Had to be her son. Maybe four years old. "What did he mean by that?"

"I don't know. He won't answer my calls and hasn't been seen since for me to ask him." She took the phone and shut off the screen. "I called in a favor from a friend stationed on base and downloaded the GPS data from Bennett's phone. His last reported location was that house."

"Family? Friends? Girlfriend? Kids?" Despite his gut instincts, her partner's disappearance might not have anything to with the assignment that'd brought them to Anchorage at all. Could've been a breakdown, a piece of Sergeant Spencer's past his partner or the army knew nothing about. Elliot Dunham's earlier observation soured on his tongue. This whole disappearing act might've been set up by Bennett himself, a way to get him out of trouble. Wouldn't be the first time he'd seen enlisted soldiers leave their post.

"No. He didn't have anyone as far as I know, but he hasn't been acting like himself since we got here. Closed off. Showing up late to work if he shows up at all." Glennon shook her head as she leaned back in the chair. "Unfortunately, our assignments don't really let us keep in contact with many people outside of work."

That meant Sergeant Spencer had no one to come looking for him. Except Glennon.

"I'm out of leads." Disappointment clouded her normally bright gaze. "I'm worried he's gotten in over his head with something."

"You want to go back to that house to find the shooter who put a bullet in you." Not a question. He could read her intentions in the way she rubbed at the hole in her shoulder. The plan made sense. Despite the fact that the idea of her stepping foot in that house hiked his pulse higher, it was their best lead to finding her partner.

Then again, Anthony wanted—no, *needed*—to hunt down the bastard who'd ambushed them, too. One way or another, he'd even the score.

"I don't think someone taking shots at me tonight

was a coincidence, and I don't think you do, either."
She had that right, but chances of the shooter staying behind after they'd high-tailed it out of there
were slim.

"I know things—" she laced her fingers together
and set her elbows against her knees "—didn't end
well… But I'm hoping we can move past this awkwardness—or whatever it is—between us. I can only
imagine how much you hate me for leaving, but I appreciate your help." A half-smile pulled at one corner
of her mouth. "Truce?"

"I don't hate you, Glennon. Trust me, I've tried."
The words were out of his mouth before he had a
chance to think about their meaning. But it was the
truth. Anthony leaned back in the office chair, his
shoulder holster and Beretta within reach on the
countertop. "Tell me about the work you two have
been doing. Is there a chance someone—a suspect—
might be looking for payback from one of your investigations?"

"Bennett and I have been partners for over three
years. We've worked a lot of investigations together.
If one of those is the starting-off point, I couldn't tell
you which one." Glennon wiped her palms down
the legs of her blood-spotted jeans. "And I've been
through them all. Several times. Nothing has stuck
out."

"Then tell me about your current investigation,"
he said.

"For the past year we've been looking into dozens of individual thefts of military weapons off army bases around the country. Most recently, a shipment of hardware has disappeared right here out of Anchorage. Usually, within a couple weeks, the weapons turn up on the black market or in the hands of our enemies, but not this time. Not a single weapon registered as stolen has turned up, which made us think whoever took them might be sticking around."

Glennon swiped the tip of her tongue across her bottom lip, running one hand through her hair before sitting forward again. "So, about two months ago, Bennett had the idea of mapping the locations of each theft, and checking those locations against enlisted soldiers stationed there at the same time. Only one name kept coming up. Staff Sergeant Nicholas Mascaro. It was a huge win for the army. After Bennett and I turned in our report and handed over all the evidence we'd collected, Nicholas Mascaro was court-martialed and convicted."

"I heard about the investigation against Mascaro." Even after leaving the military, he still had contacts. Although, he hadn't known she'd been involved so closely in the staff sergeant's arrest. A swell of pride rushed through him and he straightened a bit more. She was a damn fine investigator, no doubt about it. But something didn't sit right. Anthony thought back to his source. "But there's no way one man could run that kind of operation on his own."

"You're right." Glennon sat back in her chair. "Despite what Bennett and I wrote in our report, the army couldn't definitively tie anyone else to the staff sergeant, let alone place him at the head of the entire operation. And he's not giving up any names. So Mascaro made a deal and the investigation was officially closed."

Confusion furrowed his brow. "Then why are you and your partner here?"

"A second shipment of weapons was stolen from JBER three days ago. After Nicholas Mascaro was arrested. Bennett believed someone took control of the operation while their patsy took the fall." Glennon stood. Collecting his weapon and holster from the countertop to her right, she offered it to him, grip first. "And I think he was trying to tell me he found the proof."

THE HOUSE HADN'T changed in the last two hours, aside from the extra bullet holes peppering the walls. Fresh blood spatters added to the stains on the west side of the living room. Her blood. The hole in her shoulder ached as if to remind her of the last time she'd stood in this spot. Her attention slid to Anthony as he riffled through a stack of old newspapers, the muscles along his back hardening with every move. If he hadn't been there...

Memories of her four-year-old flashed across her

mind like lightning. His blond hair, his perfect smile, the way he'd held on to her so tight before she'd left.

Hunter was fine. He was safe. She'd made sure of it. And if anything did happen to her, he'd be cared for. Arranging his future in case something happened to her had been the only way she could track down Bennett without the army at her disposal.

Glennon ignored the tightness in her throat as she wiped at her face with the back of her hand. He was fine.

Focus. There had to be some kind of evidence pointing to the reason Bennett had come here. She kicked at a loose floorboard, but the space underneath had either never been used or been emptied out. They'd been here an hour and come up with nothing. No bullet casings. No new skid marks on the road aside from theirs. Nothing from the neighbors. Whoever had taken those shots had been either a professional or a soldier.

Glennon laughed to herself. She was getting ahead of herself. They had nothing tying Bennett's disappearance to her current investigation or the military. For all she knew, he'd needed a couple days away from the pressure of the marshal breathing down their necks for results. Her gut instincts said they were connected, but the courts didn't prosecute based off something that couldn't be proved.

"Anything on your side?" she asked.

"Not yet." Straightening, Anthony stretched to

his full, muscular height. The beginnings of sunrise glinted off a thin sheen of sweat across his forehead as he ran a hand down his face. He'd come prepared. Well, more prepared than usual. The Beretta in his shoulder holster had a couple new friends hidden in his cargo pants, his Kevlar vest, even the holster strapped around his thigh. He wasn't about to be taken by surprise again. "You?"

She studied him from the safe distance she'd decided to put between them back in the medical suite. At least three feet of space separating them at all times. That'd be the only way she could think straight during their time together. Although, now that she watched him, her body urged her to close that space. Five tours in extreme conditions ranging from jungle to desert hadn't taken away from his overall attractiveness. Hardened him, yes, but not in a bad way. And damn if that didn't resurrect some of those feelings she'd buried. But she hadn't come back here to make the same mistakes. She hadn't even planned on seeing him at all during her assignment on JBER.

"Glennon?" The weight of those dark blue eyes pinned her to the spot.

"No. Nothing." Glennon sank against one wall, exhaustion pulling at her. She wiped a bead of sweat off her neck. What were they supposed to do now? She had zero jurisdiction off base as long as Bennett's disappearance was considered a simple miss-

ing persons case. And she couldn't bring in the local
police. Not yet. Not until she could guarantee her
name would be left out of the reports. "Has your
computer expert come back with a history on this
place yet? Who owns it?"

"Last time I checked in, Elizabeth was working
her way through an entire network of shell corpora-
tions without any end in sight," he said.

Defeat spread fast. Her partner had been here.
How could he disappear without anything to show
for it? This couldn't be it. She'd been trained for
this. She couldn't have failed him already. Stalking
across the empty living room, she picked up an old
two-by-four covered in spider webs. "There has to
be something here."

She shoved every ounce of energy into her swing.
The board vibrated in her hands with each strike,
pain exploding through her shoulder. She didn't care.
Pins and needles crawled up her arms as mildewed
drywall peeled away from the wall, but she wouldn't
stop. Not until she found a clue.

"Glennon." The concern in Anthony's tone tunneled deep into her bones, but she only pushed herself harder.

She wasn't leaving this house until she had proof
Bennett had been here. It was the only lead she had.
He was the only person who could help her bring
down the rest of Staff Sergeant Mascaro's team. Another streak of sweat slipped from her hairline and

down her neck. Why was it so damn hot in here? Shouldn't the gas company have turned off the furnace when the house was abandoned?

A calloused grip encased her hands from behind, his arms caging her against a wall of muscle. Anthony turned her into him and Glennon froze. The lines at the edges of his eyes creased as he stared down at her. His grip still wrapped around hers, he studied her with determination etched into his features. "We're going to find your partner. I promise."

Promises. What good were they when nobody lived up to them? Glennon nodded, her attention wandering to the condensation building on the large front window. "It's twenty degrees outside. Nobody has lived in this house for years." The two-by-four grew heavy in her hold. She dropped it to her side but didn't let go. "Why is it so hot in here?"

"Because someone turned on the furnace." The revelation hardened Anthony's expression. He stepped away, surveying the rest of the room before unholstering the Beretta at his side. Checking the magazine, he chambered a round into the barrel. The action, so simple, forced her to swallow the tightness in her throat. This was what he did best, what she'd tracked him down for, but the sudden change consuming him from head to toe urged her to take a step back. She'd read his classified files. She understood what the "Grim Reaper" was capable of and a shiver ran through her. "Stay behind me."

"What makes you think you get to have all the fun?" Setting the two-by-four on the moldy carpeting as quietly as she could, Glennon took his left side as she withdrew her service weapon. One bullet. That was all it'd take to seal her and her partner's fates. The army would court-martial Bennett for going MIA, no matter what his reason, and drag her through the mud alongside him. She shifted her finger off the safety. Couldn't happen.

They moved as one, just as they had when he'd gotten her out of the house the first time, her steps in sync with his. Nervous energy skittered up her spine. She'd gone into plenty of dangerous situations like this before. Soldiers-turned-criminals, bullets, blood. Every investigation she'd worked had left its own mark. It was part of the job. But moving along this hallway, with *him* by her side, sent a tingling sensation down her spine that she hadn't felt in a long time.

Moonlight filtered through broken windows and bullet holes the shooter had added to the walls, playing across Anthony's face as he stalked through the house. For such a large man, he barely made a sound. He motioned with two fingers to their right. The signal was clear. They'd reached the stairs leading to the basement. And whoever had turned on the furnace after the shootout could still be down there.

Anticipation hummed through her veins. Glock raised to eye level, she fought off the shot of pain spreading through her shoulder. She was ready. This was it. With a single nod, Glennon took the first step. The unfinished wood groaned under her weight, and she paused to listen. No movement below. Nothing to suggest they were in for another ambush, but she wouldn't relax just yet. She'd had too many close calls already. Her mouth dried up; her breathing became shallow.

She paused on the last step, nothing but darkness ahead. Something brushed across her right side. Anthony. His clean, masculine scent filled her lungs, and she surveyed the full unfinished basement before they made their next move. But something charred and rotten replaced his scent within a few seconds of her hitting the bottom stair. She covered her mouth and nose in the crook of her elbow. "I recognize that smell."

She'd come across it only once since she'd been with the Military Police. An arson investigation at Pope Army Airfield in North Carolina, one of her first for the army. The fire had consumed an entire C-130J Hercules plane right before takeoff. The pilot had been sealed in the cockpit after an altercation with another airman. The smell. That was what she remembered most. "Charred remains."

Reaching for the flashlight strapped into her Kevlar vest, she brought it to life and swept the beam across the floor. Large boot prints had been preserved in a thin layer of dust. Fresh, from the look of it. But the uneven lines beside them? Those were drag marks.

A groan interrupted the heavy silence and they swung their weapons to the left in tandem. Anthony's boots hit solid cement. Weapon aimed high, he moved farther into the darkness.

Dread sank like a stone to the bottom of Glennon's stomach as she followed suit.

A click of his flashlight expanded their visibility, but only slightly. There were still three other corners of the room they couldn't see, but her gut told her whoever had turned on the furnace had disappeared long before they'd showed up. Still, she couldn't shake the vein of ice working its way up her throat. Whatever was down here—whatever they found— would make or break her investigation into Bennett's disappearance.

They reached the furnace as it kicked on for another round, the struggling mechanical groan raising the hairs on the back of Glennon's neck.

Holstering his weapon, Anthony ran his fingers over the side of the unit then lowered his flashlight beam to the floor. Four screws had fallen into the dust building up around the furnace. Glennon holstered her own gun as he handed her the flashlight. The reverberation of metal on cement as he set the panel down vibrated through her. A rush of foul air hit her hard and she buried her mouth and nose into her elbow. Anthony did the same, reaching into the unit with his free hand.

His mountainous physique blocked her view into the blackened depths. "Can you see anything?"

"Yep." A hiss escaped from between his teeth. He turned toward her, the burned remnants of a rifle highlighted by the flashlight beam. "What's left of a Heckler & Koch G28 sniper rifle. Still hot, too. Safe to assume it's the same model used to put a bullet in your shoulder three hours ago."

"The shooter tried to clean up his mess by destroying the gun in the furnace." Not a bad idea. But that left them no closer to recovering her partner. Unless… Hope spread through her chest as she stepped closer to him. "You're the weapons expert. Do you think any fingerprints survived to track down the owner?"

Leaving the rifle inside, Anthony shifted out of her way so she could see the rest of the furnace, both flashlights highlighting what else had been stuffed inside. "Looks like we already found him."

Chapter Three

Red-and-blue patrol lights deepened the shadows under Glennon's eyes as she watched the scene from the SUV. When was the last time she'd slept? Twenty-four hours ago? More? He couldn't imagine the thoughts running through her head as the remains of her best lead were loaded into the back of the coroner's van.

Anthony had kept her name out of his statement to Anchorage PD after he'd put in the initial call about an incinerated body in the furnace. Whatever was going on here—whoever had killed the shooter who'd ambushed them—it had obviously been to keep Glennon off the investigation into her missing partner. His gaze drifted back to her. She'd been right from the start. Sergeant Spencer's disappearance had something to do with the missing shipment of weapons. Why else would a shooter try to take her out, too?

"We're done here," he told the officer. "You know

how to contact me at Blackhawk Security if you have any other questions."

He had to get her to safety, someplace off-the-grid where nobody—not even his team—could find her. Where he could protect her. Anthony maneuvered around the officer and headed for the SUV.

Glennon followed his movements slowly.

Wrenching the vehicle door open, he dropped into the driver's seat. Her sweet scent hit him hard, but he didn't try to fight it off this time. After the night they'd had, he needed that piece of her with him. He breathed her in a bit deeper. Anything to ease the tension of nearly losing her all over again tonight. Spots of blood seeped through her bandage.

"What did you tell them?" she asked.

He turned the key in the ignition. The engine growled to life and he forced his eyes to focus on the road. "That we were looking to spice things up in our sex life."

She smoothed her expression. "And they believed you?" Motioning to his clothing, she leaned against the passenger-side door. "You, in all this Kevlar, with at least three weapons strapped to your chest? They believed you?"

"Don't worry. I didn't give them your real name." In reality, Anchorage PD hadn't asked too many questions about what he'd been doing in the house at all. After what had happened back in November, they recognized him and understood what kind of work he did on a regular basis. And who he did it for. Blackhawk Security had become a company the police could rely on after its CEO, Sullivan Bishop, had taken down one of the worst stalkers in city history, a case the department had moved to the bottom of their priority list. Anthony shoved the vehicle into Drive.

"Very funny." She crossed her arms over her chest, accentuating the lean muscles through her forearms. "What are you doing? We can't leave." She surveyed the cul-de-sac as he swung the SUV around, spinning her upper body toward him from the passenger seat. Her icy glare shot through him, but he wasn't about to stop. "That body is our only lead to finding my partner. Do you trust the police to fill us in if they find something?"

"We searched every inch of that house tonight, sweetheart. What exactly are you hoping they're going to find that we couldn't?" Anthony pressed his foot down on the accelerator when they hit Spenard Thruway. "Besides, you're beat. We need to take a look at that wound again, then you're going to get some sleep while we wait for the ballistics report on that bullet to come in."

"I'm fine." She settled back into her seat. "And don't call me sweetheart. You're here to protect me while I search for Bennett. Nothing more."

"Yes, ma'am." Tightening his grip around the steering wheel, Anthony studied Westchester Lagoon as they headed south. Nothing but blackness and the hint of lapping waves stared back at him. Wasn't that just the perfect metaphor for the growing silence between him and Glennon? Damn, he'd screwed things up with her to hell and back. He should've been there for her while he'd still had the chance, should've been satisfied with what he'd done for his country the first four times instead of hopping on the next transport. Maybe then she wouldn't treat him as though he were a stranger now.

He headed farther south, out of the city. Miles of nothing but trees and starlit sky stretched out before them. It was the best place to hide. No one would be able to track them out here. And even if they did, he'd be ready. The familiar rise and fall of the south end of the Chugach Mountains indicated they were close. A few more minutes and he could relax in his own territory.

"Where are you taking me?" Her voice barely overrode the sound of the heater, and he chanced a quick glance toward her. Adrenaline could only take the human body so far, and Glennon's supply had run out. Lids closing, she fought to stay awake, but wouldn't last much longer.

"Where no one can find us." Within a few minutes, gravel crunched under the SUV's tires as he pulled into a long driveway. The cabin was dark. Isolated. And, after discovering the shooter's body in that furnace, it was the best chance they had of recovering in peace.

He pulled to a stop beside the small lakeside cabin and then unloaded his gear as she made her way inside.

Dropping everything on the floor, Anthony turned on the nearest light switch. "The place isn't much, but it's fully stocked and secure." He studied her expression, trying to read any sign of what she had planned for their next move, but she'd always kept a good handle on the thoughts running through her head. "You can take the guest room at the back. Bathroom is right next door to it. Just the one, unfortunately, so we'll have to share. I never bring anyone up here."

"Never?" She surveyed the two-bedroom, one-bathroom space then moved to the front window. "It's perfect. Suits you."

"Thanks." He liked his solitude, but liked it better with her here. Hoisting his bags over his shoulder, he felt the first effects of having gone over twenty-four hours without sleep. Her call had pulled him off another assignment, but he couldn't fault her for that. "Let me unpack my gear while you settle in, and I'll bring you something to eat in about ten minutes."

"Thank you." She forced a smile but the exhaustion weighing her down didn't let it reach her eyes. She headed for the back of the cabin empty-handed, taking nearly every ounce of his control with her. Damn, he'd missed her, and no matter how many times she reminded him nothing would happen between them again, he couldn't help but imagine what

they could've been together. Stopping shy of the hallway, Glennon turned back. "For everything."

Ten minutes later her voice stopped him just outside her cracked door, only a sliver of light spilling
into the hallway. He pushed it open a few inches.

"I know what I said." Her back was to him where
she sat on the bed, but her words registered crystal-
clear. "Things are…more complicated than I thought
they'd be here. It'll be a couple more days. Can you
please put him on the phone? I just need to hear
his voice." Dressed in a set of his oversize T-shirt
and sweats, Glennon shifted on the guest bed, head
down, legs stretched in front of her and ran her hand
through her hair. The sight rocketed his pulse into
dangerous territory. "Hey, baby." Her voice lightened in an instant, a beautiful smile spreading across
her expression. "I know. I'm sorry I woke you. I
just missed you so much. Are you being good for
Grandma?"

Anthony settled against the door frame, entranced
by the sudden shift in her mood. The plate grew
heavy in his hand, but he'd stand there all night if
there was a chance he'd get a glimpse of that smile
again.

"You went to the zoo without me? That sounds
fun. Can I call you again tomorrow so you can tell
me more about it?" Those mesmerizing green eyes
brighter than he'd ever seen, she leaned back against
the headboard and crossed her legs over the pillow

top. A laugh escaped from between her perfectly pink lips, tightening his insides. "Okay. Go back to sleep, my love. I'll see you soon."

He couldn't move. Couldn't think. In the few seconds she'd spoken to her son, he'd felt her undeniable love, and something inside him splintered. He gripped the plate hard. She would've made an amazing mother to their kids. Hell, she was obviously an amazing mother already. Couldn't even keep herself from calling her son so early in the morning. Anthony ignored the tightness in his throat and straightened. Didn't matter. She'd made it clear how their relationship would proceed. As partners. Nothing more.

With three knocks, he shouldered his way into the room with everything on a plate. "Hungry? I made your favorite. Aspirin, clean gauze and my special egg salad sandwich."

"Yeah." Glennon shot off the mattress, wiping at her face. A split second later she turned toward him again, locking down any hint of emotion. She sniffed as she maneuvered around the bed. "I'm starving. Thanks."

His stomach sank. She was getting far too skilled at hiding those emotions of hers, to the point he questioned whether he'd really seen her smile a few minutes ago. "Was it something I said?"

"What? No. It's not you. I appreciate you letting me stay here." She shook her head, a flush of pink rising in her cheeks. Her long fingers brushed against his as she reached for the plate. Heat seared through him as she took a step back and raised the plate in acknowledgment. "And for the food. I—"

"You miss your son." He'd read it in the way her skin had paled in the few short moments after she'd disconnected the call, in the way her tears had dried a path down her cheeks.

"Stupid, right? I mean, he's safe. That's all that matters. Nobody knows about him. Not the army. Not his father. I shouldn't have anything to worry about." A weak smile played across her mouth. Shoulders rising on a deep inhale, she glanced up at him, signs of her apparent misery wiped clean from her expression. "I can't tell you how much I've missed your egg salad. Every time I've tried to re-create the recipe, it turns out wrong. I finally gave up trying."

"I add hot sauce at the end." Okay. He'd pretend she hadn't let a piece of herself out into the open.

Anthony backed toward the hallway, reaching for the doorknob to close it behind him. "Get some rest, change your gauze. The ballistics report should be here soon. We'll figure out our next move then."

"Listen, I know things are different between us now, but I've had a hell of a day." Her lips parted as she took a single step forward and, for the first time, he noted the dark swirl of purple nail polish on her bare feet. She glanced at her cell phone on the nightstand. "Hunter usually sleeps in my bed, and I won't be able to sleep unless…"

Grip tight on the doorknob, Anthony froze. Pressure built in his lungs.

She locked her gaze on him, determined, sincere. "Will you stay with me until I fall asleep?"

WHAT HAD SHE been thinking?

She hadn't. That had been one of the problems whenever Glennon was around him. She couldn't think straight. And here, in a small lakeside cabin filled with his scent, with *him* mere inches from her, she'd must've lost her damn mind. She ran her free hand through her hair, a nervous habit she'd used to try to relieve some tension over the past few years. Without success.

"You think that's a good idea?" Anthony released the door handle, his tone registering exactly how much she'd already asked of him in the last four hours. *Too much.* Especially for a man she'd walked out on while he was in the middle of serving his country, a decision she'd regret for the rest of her life.

"No." Heat rose up her neck and flooded her face. She shook her head, forcing another smile she didn't feel. Her fingers tingled, urging her to run her hand through her hair one more time, but she rolled them into a fist at her side instead. Taking another step toward him, she focused on the raised outline of a chain hidden under his shirt. Dog tags? "And I don't have any right to ask after everything you've done for me already. But the past couple days have been a nightmare and I need…I need you to stay."

Anthony swayed on his feet as though he intended to back toward the door. His full beard kept her from reading his expression entirely, but his eyes had always been the window to his thoughts. Gorgeous, dark blue eyes she'd tried for years to forget. And right now, the battle swirling in their depths was spreading across his features. His brows drew inward as he ran a hand down his beard. "Glennon—"

"Please." She fought the urge to grip his shirt to keep him from leaving. Notching her chin higher, she studied the face she'd missed since the day she'd left. "If it helps, I promise to keep my hands to myself."

"It's not your hands I'm worried about." He moved into her. A rush of his reinvigorated, clean, masculine scent filled her lungs as her brain fought to catch up. Had he showered while she'd been on the phone with Hunter? Only the thin fabric of a T-shirt she'd found in one of the dresser drawers separated them. He kept his touch light, giving her enough room to escape if she wanted to. Which she should. Because she'd most definitely violated her three-foot rule. "Do you ever think of what might've happened if you hadn't left?"

Glennon swallowed hard, her pulse pounding behind her ears as she set the plate of food, the painkillers and gauze on the bed. No point in lying. He knew her too well. She passed her tongue across her too-dry lips as he stared down at her as though she were the only woman in the world who mattered to him. "Sometimes."

All the time. The only way she'd been able to give those thoughts a break over the last five years was by throwing herself into her work and into being there for her son. Throwing herself into everything that didn't include Anthony Harris. She'd made her choice then and she stood by it now. She'd suffer the consequences, no matter how many times she'd thought of coming home. She stared at the open door behind him for a moment, into the darkness of the cabin.

"Sometimes I think I could've changed your mind, convinced you I was enough for you to stay home." The comforting warmth rolling off him in waves urged her to stay put. It'd been a long time since she'd gotten lost in somebody's touch, relied on someone other than herself. She'd almost forgotten what intimacy felt like since becoming a single mother. It'd be easy to give in to him. Right here, right now. Forget about her missing partner, forget how lonely she'd been over the last few years, and just do something for herself for a change. But extricating herself from a romantic relationship with this man had been one of the hardest things she'd ever done. Something she wasn't interested in doing again, not with Hunter involved.

"But that was a long time ago. Things have changed." Glennon stepped out of his hold, the rough calluses on his palms catching on the cotton shirt she'd borrowed. "And it finally took me leaving to realize changing your mind was one case I'd never have closure to."

Disappointment darkened his features. "You were always enough for me, Glennon. More than enough." His tone dipped into dangerous territory, raising tiny goose bumps on her arms. He countered the step she'd taken to the point where she had to stare up at him. "You were the only person who could help me forget what I'd seen every time I came home. You were the one I trusted to keep my head on straight, to bring me back to who I really was. Not the soldier. Me. You were everything."

Her knees shook, the blood drained from her face. As Military Police, she'd walked into dozens of situations more confident than she felt in this moment. This wasn't the plan. The rules had been plain. No matter how many times the past came back to haunt her, she'd keep herself in check. But now... "I didn't know that."

The muted ding from his phone released the pressure building behind her sternum. Saved by the bell. She took the opportunity to distance herself from his reach as Anthony checked the screen. Sitting on the bed, she stared down at her hands as her stomach flipped. From hunger or from the sincerity in his voice, she had no idea. Didn't matter. She could only fix one of those things at the moment. The other? Couldn't happen again. Nothing could happen between them again.

"The ballistics report came in early," he said. "Vincent's contacts in forensics were able to lift a print from the homemade bullet recovered from the windshield."

So much for getting a couple hours of sleep. Glennon shoved off from the bed, a strike of pain spreading across her shoulder. She massaged the area around the wound as she moved to view the screen. He flipped through the report too fast for her to see specifics, but one line stood out among the rest, highlighted on the phone's screen.

"Private First Class Gani Miller." The name sounded familiar on her lips. But where had she read it before?

"Left the army because of a dishonorable discharge, now makes his living as a gun for hire. Paid to take you out." Anthony swiped his thumb across the screen to the next page. "I'll have Elizabeth look into his financials to find out who hired him."

Glennon stayed put as he called the former NSA consultant. Mentally sifting through her investigations for the army, she studied the recliner tucked into the corner of the room, but couldn't really focus on anything in particular. Where had she heard that name before? A shooter for hire had most likely made his way to the top of her Most Wanted list, but that wasn't it. She reviewed the list every morning before heading onto the base, and Private Gani Miller's name hadn't been on there as of yesterday. "Do you have a laptop here?"

Anthony spun toward her. "I packed one in my gear. Gray duffel bag in the hallway."

In less than two minutes she'd powered the laptop up and logged in with the username and password Anthony had written down for her while on the phone with Elizabeth. The screen came to life as she settled back on the bed.

Her heart skipped a beat.

There, in the center of the black desktop background, was a photo of…her. Smiling, arms wrapped around her brand-new fiancé. The memories of that day interrupted her concentration as she zeroed in on the yellow-gold engagement ring he'd slipped onto her finger moments before the photo had been taken. She'd set that same ring on the kitchen counter as she'd walked out the door for the last time five years ago. What had he done with it?

"All right." Anthony disconnected his call. "Elizabeth is pulling everything she can find on Gani Miller as we speak. Still nothing leading back to who owns that house, though."

Panic flooded through her. Glennon rushed to bring up the backup of her investigation files. The mattress dipped as he sat beside her. She swallowed hard then typed the shooter's name into the search bar. No point in bringing up the past. They had more important things to worry about now. "I know I've heard that name before. If Private Miller has been at this for a while, he might be linked to one of my investigations."

The fact the sniper had been military couldn't have been a coincidence.

The search of her files came up blank.

Her eyebrows drew together. She checked that she'd spelled the shooter's name correctly and pushed Enter a second time. Nothing. There had to be some connection. "That's weird. I know I've come across that name before."

"Are you remembering it from somewhere else?" Anthony leaned into her to get a clear shot of the screen. His powerful, muscled thigh brushed against her, and she licked her lips.

"I don't know where else…" A single image of handwritten notes flashed across her mind. "That's it." Glennon checked another file, one she'd been compiling since her partner had gone missing.

"After Bennett disappeared, I searched his barracks and found a bunch of notes he'd scribbled on napkins he'd left in the trash bin. Most of it was nonsense, but that name—Gani Miller—was on one of the napkins with a few others." She reentered her username and password to access the secure files. "I took pictures of them in case something led to

Bennett's whereabouts, and uploaded the photos to my online storage."

A new rush of hope blossomed in the center of her chest. They had a name, a lead. She could find Bennett and get back to her life. Back to her son. Double clicking the track pad, Glennon leaned away from the laptop. No. No, no, no, no. Her throat tightened. "That's not possible."

"What's not possible?" Anthony shifted the computer out of her lap and onto his own. With a few clicks of the track pad, he stroked his beard. Confusion swept across his features. "Where are the files?"

"They were there. I backed up my files from my laptop to this drive in case something happened and I couldn't get to my computer." Which probably meant... Glennon stood, crossing the room to the pile of clothing she'd discarded on the floor.

"And now they're gone," he said. "How?"

"Someone accessed my backup and deleted them." She stripped out of the borrowed sweats then pushed her legs into her jeans, all thoughts of privacy retreating to the back of her mind. Nobody knew about those files. How had evidence catalogs, Bennett's investigation notes, witness statements and photographs of the napkins all disappeared overnight?

"And I think I know where they're going next."

Chapter Four

"Where the hell do you think you're going?" He wasn't about to let her walk into another ambush, even with the possibility of finding her partner. "You haven't slept in who knows how long, you're running on empty, and there's blood dripping down your shirt. You're going to crash any second. You need—"

"What I need is to find Bennett." Glennon turned her back to him while she crossed her arms under the oversize T-shirt and brought it over her head. Shadows played across her lean back as she bent for her clothing. Blood spotted the gauze taped across the backside of her wound, but his attention shot to the raised lump of scar tissue over her ribs, the one paler than the rest of her skin. The one that looked strangely like another bullet wound. She'd been shot before?

Glennon faced him, pulling the shirt she'd borrowed from Elizabeth over her head. "Everything I had in those backups came from Bennett. He's the only one who can prove Staff Sergeant Mascaro's operation has been taken over by a new leader. And there's only one place someone could've accessed those files to delete them."

"What is that?" He nodded toward her, each word tearing from him. "That scar on your back. Where did it come from?"

She froze, spine a bit straighter. She placed her boots on the bed carefully, slowly. "Thought you'd recognize an old bullet wound when you saw one, Ranger. Don't you have a few of these yourself?"

"When?" Anthony didn't blink, didn't move. Any second now his control would shatter. Someone had shot her and she hadn't said a word, hadn't reached out to him before now? He wanted details. A name. Whoever had pulled that trigger would wish they hadn't. "Who?"

"Doesn't matter. Reliving old investigations isn't going to help me find my partner any faster, and that's what I hired you to do." She reached for her boots and sat on the edge of the bed, lacing them quickly. The blazing determination in her expression said she wasn't going to see reason. In the end, it didn't matter what he said to convince her otherwise. It wouldn't work. Once she set her sights on something, the devil himself couldn't stop her. That was one of the things he'd loved about her. Glennon headed to the door, wiping a strand of hair out of her face without glancing back at him.

But she wasn't getting away that easily. Anthony crossed the room in three strides and wrapped a hand around her arm. Spinning her into him, he filled the door frame. She wanted to leave? She'd have to go through him, and he wasn't moving until she told him the truth. "What's so damn important about this case that you're willing to put your own well-being at risk?"

"Because it's my last." She visibly flinched at the words, something he'd never witnessed before. Her sudden reaction lightened his grasp on her arm. Either her words had hit a sore spot or Glennon was far more exhausted than she wanted to admit.

He released his hold as pressure built in his gut. "What do you mean?"

"When this is over—" she pulled back her shoulders "—after I recover Bennett, I'm putting in my papers for discharge."

"You love your job." Anthony gave her another foot of space. He'd followed her career from the start. Processing crime scenes on bases, illegal dealings across state lines, all those soldiers she'd helped. She'd spent the last decade studying, working for a cause she believed in. And she was damn good at it. What could've possibly changed? "You've made a difference. Why would you want to leave?"

The answer sat on the tip of his tongue before she even said a word.

"Hunter." The glassy haze over her eyes revealed she wasn't really seeing him in front of her. "When

I was shot last year…" She shifted on her feet. "He's four years old. He's already had to live without a father in his life. He deserves to grow up with a mother who isn't risking her life on the job or who might not come home at all." A thin smile curved one side of her mouth as she lifted her eyes to his. "I love my job, and I think I'm good at it, but I love him more. And I want to see him grow up. I want to see school pictures, watch him fall in love for the first time, get married. Have a family of his own someday."

She rolled her lips between her teeth and turned her face away. As if she needed to hide from him. "Sounds silly when I say it out loud. Me, giving up the past ten years of my life. But sacrifice is part of the job, right? That's what I agreed to when I decided to keep him after I found out I was pregnant. I just honestly didn't think this day would come."

"It's not silly." Anthony slid his hands around to her lower back, drawing her into him. Surprisingly, she let him. The muscles down her spine stiffened, but inch by inch they released as he held her. Her rosy scent drifted from her hair as she closed her eyes. Rose oil had always been one of her favorite natural perfumes.

She pressed her cheek into his chest, right over his heart. Still a perfect fit. Then again, he'd always believed she'd been created just for him. "But as much as you want to finish this investigation, you're not going anywhere until you've had a couple hours of sleep."

"What?" She stepped back.

"You hired me to protect you." He framed her face between his calloused hands. Rough against smooth perfection. Dark versus light. "If my legacy is to step in front of a bullet for you, so be it. That's my job. But I can't do that job if you're determined to destroy yourself first."

Her lips parted. She was beautiful. Absolutely, gut-wrenchingly beautiful. Always had been. Always would be, to him. But the small burst of a smile didn't reach her eyes; rather, it merely accentuated the hollowness and exhaustion etched into her features.

She pointed at the window and stepped out of his hold, one hand on his chest. "You want me to catch up on my sleep while Bennett's out there, possibly dead?"

"You aren't good to anyone in your current condition, especially your partner, and we aren't going to solve anything unless you have a clear head." Anthony countered her escape, his voice dropping as he backed her to the end of the bed. "So to answer your question, yes. Right now, the most useful thing you can do for your partner is get some rest."

Her knees hit the bed frame and she collapsed onto the mattress. Pink flared in her cheeks. She rubbed at her left temple. "You're probably right. I can barely see straight. But the files—"

"Will still be deleted when you wake up." He leaned forward, boxing her in with his arms as he gripped a pillow behind her. His mouth mere centimeters from hers, he shoved the memory of her taste, the feel of her lips on his, down deep. No matter how much he wanted to close that small space between them, he wouldn't violate her request to keep their relationship professional.

Heat spread through his chest as her sharp exhale slid across his throat. He should go. Peeling himself away from her, away from her raw, warm energy, he handed her the pillow. "Don't worry. I'll watch over you."

"I have no doubt." She settled back against the mattress, fully dressed, as he took a seat in the recliner across the room.

Within minutes her breathing slowed, barely audible over the pounding behind his ears. Her expression was relaxed, no longer hollow and controlled, the stress all but gone.

The nightstand lamp reflected off a hint of metal protruding from under the edge of her pillow, right near her hand. Anthony crossed the room, his mouth pulling tight to one side. A blade. But not just any blade. A combat blade he'd brought home from Iraq. The one he'd given her for their two-year anniversary. He studied the angles of her cheekbones, his fingers tingling to brush away a strand of stray hair that'd fallen across her face. As much as she'd made it clear she wouldn't acknowledge their past, the blade proved she'd obviously had a hard time cutting those emotional ties.

His hand trailed to the chain stashed under his shirt collar. Then again, so had he. He moved back to the recliner, the Beretta in his shoulder holster digging into his side.

It had already started, his getting wrapped up in her again. And it hadn't even taken a full day. He'd invested hundreds of hours into his training. Weapons and explosives, interrogation, recovery, extraction, capture. All of it had been for nothing when it came to her. She'd blown past his defenses—circumvented the walls he'd built—with four simple words. *I need your help.* Damn, he was a sucker for pain. Because that was the only way this could go. In the end, whether they found her partner or not, Glennon would go back to her life when this was over. She'd move on. Again. And he'd be left to pick up the pieces. Again.

Exhaustion pulled him deeper into the chair. He'd been trained to sleep with one eye open— never knew when or where an attack would come. The intel he'd requested from Elizabeth about the shooter who'd tried to kill Glennon wouldn't be in for a few more hours. He'd set the security system and restocked his ammunition before bringing her the sandwich. If anyone came after her again, he'd be more than ready.

She was safe. He'd made her a promise and he'd be damned sure he kept it.

"Good night, sweetheart." He might be a sucker for pain, but for him, any small amount of Glennon would be worth a thousand bullet wounds.

A SOFT CREAK reached his ears. Anthony unholstered his gun automatically as he flipped his watch for the time. He'd taken position in the chair two hours ago. Pinks and oranges bled through the thick curtains. Sunrise. His heart pounded hard in his chest as he surveyed the room. Glennon hadn't moved from the bed, but had rolled onto her side sometime while he'd been asleep. He slid out of the chair, cocking his ear toward the door. Nothing.

But it hadn't been nothing. That creak. He'd heard it. And the only spot in the cabin where the floorboards protested like that was right in front of the bathroom, mere feet from this room.

Someone had broken into the house.

With one last glance at Glennon, Anthony gripped the doorknob. He slipped into the hallway and closed the door behind him. His eyes adjusted to the darkness fast, every instinct on high alert.

From the center of the hallway, the shadowed intruder widened his stance. "You can't protect her from what's coming."

Anthony raised his gun and took aim. "Watch me."

TWO GUNSHOTS EXPLODED through the darkness.

Glennon rocketed out of bed, wrapping one hand around the combat blade she'd stashed under her pillow and the other around her service weapon on the nightstand. The room was empty, her panicked breathing blocking any hint of sound outside her closed bedroom door. "Anthony?"

He wasn't there.

She rushed into the hallway. Swinging her weapon up to shoulder height, she forced her heartbeat to slow as her eyes adjusted to the darkness. Listen. Breathe.

Glennon hugged the wall as she moved, one foot in front of the other. The floorboard in front of the bathroom protested under her weight with a groan, and she froze. Nothing. No sign of movement anywhere in the house. No other shots fired. Had she dreamed the whole thing?

Glennon cleared the cabin room by room, the hairs on the back of her neck standing on end. No. Those shots had been all too real, and the fact that Anthony wasn't in the cabin screamed something had gone wrong.

Morning streams of sunrise intensified a shadow as it rushed past the largest window in the front room.

She swung the Glock around, finger beside the trigger. A rush of freezing Alaskan air caught in her throat. The front door was open. She ran her tongue across her dry lips. She'd taken a killing shot once before. If something had happened to Anthony…

No. She had to focus. He could take care of himself. Hell, the Rangers had given him a nickname that only brushed the surface of his capabilities. The blade she'd stuffed into the waistband of her jeans cut against her skin as she forced herself out onto the porch. Pink-and-orange rays of sunrise highlighted the short expanse from the cabin to Campbell Lake, but nothing more. Nobody on the pier, nothing but fishing boats docked at the edge of the water. A thin line of trees surrounded the property, but nothing moved.

Damn it. Where was he?

"Anthony!" She took a single step off the porch. Her ears strained for a hint of what might be waiting for her, only the lapping of soft waves fighting for her attention. The gun grew heavy in her grasp. Something was wrong. He wouldn't just leave. He wouldn't abandon her.

A roughened palm clamped over her mouth, another around the barrel of the Glock. Ripping it from her grasp, her attacker tossed the gun to the ground, out of reach.

Her head slammed back into his shoulder as he lifted her off her feet. A scream worked up her throat. She swung her momentum forward to un-balance him, but his hold wouldn't loosen. His hand slipped from her mouth. *The knife.* If she could get to the blade…

"You're going to stop looking for your partner, Sergeant Chase." His rough growl vibrated through her. "Before you get yourself and the people you care about killed."

Her spine seized. The people she cared about… Hunter.

"If you go near him, I will kill you." Glennon rammed her elbow into her attacker's solar plexus, and went for the knife stuffed inside the waistband of her jeans. In a single movement, she arced the blade up and back over her shoulder. His hand disappeared from around her waist as she swung at his collar. But missed. He'd jumped back from her and she dived for the gun. Landing hard, she knocked the icy breath from her lungs and slid her finger over the trigger. She hiked the gun over her shoulder and fired. The gun kicked back in her hand.

But he was gone.

The corner of the cabin ruptured in splinters from her shot. The bullet had missed its mark. Glennon surveyed the rest of the porch, the pier, the thin line of trees surrounding the property. He'd disappeared.

"Glennon!" Anthony's concern carried across the property as he ran out of the tree line toward her.

He darted past the corner of the house, gun in hand, after her attacker.

Her breath sawed in and out of her lungs. Shoving to her feet, she gripped her weapon and gave chase. She pumped her legs hard. The bastard had threatened her son. He wasn't getting away.

More than thirty yards ahead, the figure dressed in head-to-toe black and a ski mask ripped open the door to a waiting pickup. They were going to lose him. Desperation dumped another round of adrenaline into her blood.

Her attacker raised his weapon. In a split second both she and Anthony had been placed on the wrong side of the gun. But Anthony didn't stop. Two shots kicked up dirt and snow at his feet, but he kept advancing.

"Anthony, no!" Rushing forward, she put herself between him and the chance of high-speed lead poisoning, just as he'd done for her back at the abandoned house. She shot her hands up, her gun pointed at the brightening sky in surrender. She wouldn't risk Anthony taking a bullet for her, no matter how used to the idea he'd become. Puffs of air crystalized in front of her lips, but she couldn't move—couldn't think—as her attacker climbed into the truck and turned over the engine. Anthony's chest pressed into her uninjured shoulder, as though she was the only barrier holding him back.

Within seconds the truck tires kicked up gravel at the end of the property, and her attacker disappeared.

Her hands ached from gripping her weapon so damn tight. A rush of defeat flooded through her. She collapsed onto her knees, every ounce of energy draining from her. It'd been a warning. Despite hitting dead end after dead end, she'd somehow gotten close. Why else would someone break in? The intruder's words registered as her nervous system returned to normal. *You're going to stop looking for your partner.*

She wasn't the hiding type. She'd fight. She'd find Bennett, and she'd protect her son. Snow worked its way through her socks, but the sharp pain in one knee pulled at her focus. She'd hit something. Moving her knee, Glennon focused on the small metal pin reflecting the final stages of purple-and-blue Alaskan sunrise.

An American flag pin.

"You okay?" Anthony's boots appeared in her peripheral vision as he closed in on her. "Did he hurt you?"

A chill swept across her back the longer she studied the pin. "No. I'm…fine."

"Bastard disabled my security system. He ran into the tree line and doubled back." Rage darkened Anthony's voice as he crouched beside her. He lowered his voice. "I heard another gunshot."

"I shot at him." Glennon curled her fingers into

her palm, the sharp edge of the pin digging into her skin. She'd taken the shot. Shoving off the ground, she took a full breath of cold morning air to clear her head. Didn't work. Nothing but tracking down her partner would. "We need to get to my barracks."

"Someone just attacked you. Every second you're out in the open, you're at risk." Anthony raised the Beretta he'd relied on for so long, using it to point to the location the pickup—and their attacker—had disappeared. The furrow between his brows deepened as anger sparked in his eyes. "That sniper who put a bullet in your shoulder was a professional, sweetheart. That bastard who just bypassed my security system? A professional. These guys aren't messing around. You're not safe, and I will not lose you a second time."

Shock beat through her and Glennon swallowed hard. The swooping of a bald eagle along the tree line pulled her back into the moment. Her missing partner. The fact someone had broken into the cabin to threaten her. The shot she'd taken. "Then it's a good thing I hired a Ranger to protect me."

"Glennon…" he said.

No. They weren't doing this. She couldn't.

"I hid the hard copies of the files that were deleted off my backup in my barracks." She leveled her chin with the ground. Wood splintered off the spot where her bullet had penetrated the corner of the cabin. Her attacker was gone, his warning crystal-clear in her head. She tucked the combat blade into her left boot. Her hands shook, even with one wrapped around the grip of her gun, and before she understood what was happening, Anthony had encased them in his grasp. His heat penetrated the thick haze of her last few minutes.

If she was being honest with herself, she'd missed this. Missed him. Because even though Anthony Harris had been nicknamed the Grim Reaper by his superiors, he'd always held the skills to bring her to life. Even after she wasn't his anymore. She might've needed a bit of that warmth right now, but she slid her hands out of his. "We should get going."

Stepping away from her, Anthony extended his hand toward the cabin. It was hard to read his expression. Tight. Hollow. Jaw clenched. As though he were locking down the emotions burning through him as she had so many times around him. "Lead the way, Sergeant."

Sergeant. Not sweetheart.

Glennon brushed past him, her stomach heavy. Her attacker had threatened her son. Wrong choice. He'd known who she was, knew of the people she cared about. He should've killed her when he'd had the chance. If anything happened to her son now, she wouldn't hesitate like he had. A threat to back off the investigation and a single warning shot. That'd been it. He was lucky that was as far as it'd gotten. Still, none of it made sense.

She froze.

"He's been watching me." How else could her attacker have found her so quickly? The dull ache in her wrists from the gun's kickback intensified as a shudder raced through her. The thought of being watched—stalked—tightened every muscle she had. What else had the intruder compiled on her? Her memory drifted to the conversation with her son. What was this guy willing to use against her to back off the search for her partner?

She spun into Anthony. "Watching us."

"I will find him, Glennon." The rage tightening the tendons between his neck and shoulders disintegrated the second he set sights on her, the growl from his voice disappearing. "You don't have to be afraid."

"I'm not afraid. He warned me to back off. He threatened me and the people I care about. If anybody is going to find him, it's me." The American flag pin in her pocket demanded attention. She rolled back her injured shoulder. Pain zinged through the wound like lightning, but it only solidified her determination and cleared her head. "I don't care what that bastard said. Those files are the only lead to finding Bennett and putting an end to this nightmare. And I'm going to see this through to the end."

Chapter Five

Her attacker had gotten close to her. Touched her.

Pain radiated through Anthony's knuckles and into his shoulders from his clenching his fists so hard. He didn't care. He could've lost her this morning. Again.

Rolling his head back onto his shoulders, he mentally counted to ten. Two attempts on her life in two days. So far he'd done a bang-up job of keeping her safe. He ran a hand through his beard. How had that bastard gotten past his security system in the first place?

The soldier stationed at the entrance to the base reviewed their credentials.

"Welcome to JBER, Sergeant Major Harris, Sergeant Chase." The soldier handed back their ID. "Weapons, please. You can retrieve them when you leave."

Glennon and Anthony both handed over their handguns, saluted and then drove straight for the barracks. Pulling into the lot, she shoved the SUV into Park, but didn't move to get out. "All right. You haven't said a word since we left the cabin, and I'm starting to think it has something to do with what happened this morning."

Her sarcasm wouldn't lighten his mood.

"You could've been killed." The words ripped from his throat. How could he have been so careless as to follow those tracks? The second her attacker had taken off for the trees, he should've known the bastard would double back to get to his target: Glennon. Anthony locked his jaw, the ache at the base of his skull intensifying as they stepped from the vehicle.

"But I wasn't." She closed the self-imposed distance between them as she rounded the front of the SUV, slipping her hand across his arm. A rush of electricity shot through him. After all these years apart, how could she still affect him like this? "If you hadn't been there to head that guy off in the hallway, who knows what would've happened. You saved my life whether you want to see it that way or not."

He wasn't sure about that. Her attacker had had her within his reach, could've ended it right then, yet he'd run for the pickup. Glennon's relayed warning had echoed through his mind since leaving the cabin. What if they were coming at Sergeant Bennett's disappearance all wrong?

She dropped her hold, heading inside, and he inhaled sharply to steady himself. Tan paint, white tile, an endless hallway and heavy steel doors. Just as he remembered, although he'd only been stationed here a few weeks before shipping out. Anthony missed the weight of his Beretta as they moved toward her room. Chances of needing it on base were slim, but the thought of someone gunning for her grated on his nerve endings.

"Home sweet home." She dangled the key between her index finger and thumb then handed it off. No physical contact this time. "Try not to make a mess. I have inspections when my leave ends in three days."

He slid the key into the door and twisted, shouldering his way inside. After flipping the light switch, he stepped back into the hallway. "Whoever searched your room before we got here obviously didn't get the memo."

"What?" Glennon pushed past him.

Her room had been trashed. Feathers from slashed pillows nearly covered the floor, while holes in walls crumbled drywall onto the ripped sheets. Whoever had broken into Glennon's room had been searching for something. Anthony focused the lingering rage climbing up his throat into searching for the files. It'd been a damn good thing she hadn't been anywhere near here.

He hugged the wall, moving through the room one step at a time. No movement. No intruders hiding under the twin-size bed or in the wood cabinets where her uniforms and civilian clothing spilled out onto the tile. His instincts said whoever had caused this mess had taken off a while ago. Could've been the same person who'd taken care of the shooter back at the abandoned house. The same person who'd broken into the cabin? That gave them at least a two-hour head start.

Every cabinet had been opened, every couch cushion destroyed. No stone left unturned. But Anthony read no real organization in the search. It had been disorganized, frenzied. The shooter who'd put a bullet in her shoulder had been a professional. The man at the cabin? Also a professional. This was… something else. Desperation.

"Well, I think I'm definitely going to fail inspection." Glennon ran a hand through her hair, collapsing onto the edge of her mattress. The small muscles along her jaw tightened. She tried to hide her reaction, but hints of disbelief bled through her stony features—the slight widening of her eyes, the way she rolled her fingers into the center of her palm. She kicked personal items out of her way. Some clothing, a toothbrush, a broken compact mirror. "The only reason someone would've done this was to look for the hard copies of those files deleted off my backup."

And it had to be someone enlisted. There was no other way they could've gotten on base.

"Where are they?" Anthony nodded at the hole

in the back of the cabinet, the perfect size and shape for a wall safe. Although, the safe had clearly been taken by the intruder in a quick getaway. Interrupted during their search? Before they left he'd get in touch with base security to check the security footage. Not a whole lot of places a soldier could disappear with a wall safe in tow.

She stood, making a beeline for the bathroom. Within ten seconds Glennon reemerged, an empty manila file folder in one hand and a black laptop in the other. She tossed the folder onto the floor. "They got the hard copies I taped under the bathroom sink." Hiking her thumb over her shoulder, she leaned against the doorjamb. "And they destroyed my laptop. Unless your computer expert can recover a damaged hard drive, everything I had on Bennett's disappearance is gone."

"I'll have Sullivan call in Captain Reise to start processing the scene with the base's investigative unit. She's a prosecutor stationed here at JBER, but she should have a few favors to call in." Anthony gripped his cell phone. "She might be able to tell us what our next move is."

"Do you honestly think it'll do any good? Seems like every time we get a lead, it's a dead end." Glennon tossed the battered laptop onto the bed and studied the room once more. "Whoever did this is military. And they obviously don't want me to recover Bennett. So either they have something to do with his disappearance or they're covering someone's ass. Maybe both."

Covering someone's ass. The furrow between his brows deepened. "You think this is linked to the stolen weapons shipments."

"That's my reigning theory. Bennett is smart and he's trained. He wouldn't go down easily. He sent me a message saying he had proof. Most likely proof someone had taken Staff Sergeant Mascaro's place at the head of the theft operation. Intel like that could be enough to kill for." She nodded at the shared door on the other side of the room. "Bennett's barracks are—were—right next to mine. Probably looks as good as mine does right now, too, unless the marshal has gotten to it."

"The marshal." The attacker at the cabin had known he was a Ranger, had known where to find them, had had the ability to bypass highly secure alarm systems. There were only so many people in the world who had access to that kind of intel and training. "I'd say he's a good place to start."

"You think the Provost Marshal General, a man who reports directly to the Chief of Staff of the US Army, has something to do with Bennett's disappearance?" She turned away fast, a burst of laughter escaping up her throat before she faced him again. "That's ridiculous. The marshal sent us here to investigate the stolen weapons. Why bring us here at all if he didn't want us to find the soldiers responsible?"

"To keep an eye on your work, to see what you and Bennett uncovered. And if you found something he didn't like…he could get rid of the evidence." And the investigators themselves. The pieces were falling into place. Anthony didn't have the proof, but there was too much opportunity to not at least talk to the man.

"And when Bennett found proof Mascaro's operation was still going strong under new leadership, the marshal contracted a hit on both of us to tie up the loose ends." Glennon sank against the bathroom doorjamb again, her gaze locked on the laptop. She rubbed at the hole in her shoulder. Shaking her head, she shoved away from the doorway, a new shade of determination coloring her features. "Still doesn't tell us where Bennett is. If we're going to accuse the Marshal General of being involved, we need hard evidence to prove it. Irrefutable."

"Agreed." Anthony's phone buzzed in his hand. Sullivan Bishop, CEO and founder of Blackhawk Security, had gotten his significant other to agree to process the scene off the books. But he and Glennon weren't going to wait around. He'd promised to protect her during this investigation, and that was exactly what he'd do. Even if it cost him everything. "Tell me how we find him."

Glennon extracted her phone from her jacket pocket and swiped her finger across the screen. "Lieutenant General Samuel Sykes is usually stationed at CID command in Quantico, but he's decided on a more hands-on approach with this investigation. Just so happens, he's right here on base. I even have a picture." She shuffled around the bed through the debris, her boot catching on the corner of the frame. She fell forward.

Anthony moved fast, catching her before she hit the floor. He wrapped his hand around her wrist, her strong pulse beating under his touch. A flood of light pink burned into her cheeks. A rough exhale escaped from between her lips as he righted her, but he didn't let go. Her sweet rosy scent surrounded him, drawing him closer. Another bolt of electricity—stronger than before—surged through him. Damn, what her touch could do to him. Her attention drifted farther down. To the chain around his neck that had dislodged from under his T-shirt when she fell.

The one with her yellow-gold engagement ring strung through it.

HE'D KEPT IT all this time. Her ring. Not just kept it, but wore it around his neck. Glennon swallowed hard. Close to his chest.

She straightened, taking a step back. He couldn't still have feelings for her after all these years. He'd moved on. They both had. He'd gone into private security; she'd put everything she had into her career to forget him. There'd been other women for him and other men for her. Although, as she ran through the short list of dates over the past few years, she couldn't deny she'd held Sergeant Major Anthony Harris on a pedestal. He'd been her first love. Always would be. Her throat dried. "Why do you have my engagement ring?"

"I never intended for you to see that." He fisted the ring and shoved it back down his shirt. Turning away from her, Anthony moved with predatory power. He closed down his expression the same way she closed down hers when she didn't want to surrender the upper hand. Pure stone.

"That's not an answer." Her heart drummed too hard and too fast in her chest. She didn't let her expression change, but couldn't control the tingling sensation spreading down her body. A single step forward was all it took for him to face her again. "Do you…?" She licked her lips. "Have you been wearing that all this time?"

"The most important people in my life are my team." Sadness swirled in those dark blue eyes, rocketing her heart into her throat. She knew that. While on tour in Afghanistan, his entire team had been killed right in front of him. He hadn't ever given her the details, but a few calls up the chain of command had filled in the blanks. Forty-eight hours without support in enemy territory. And he'd made it out alive. Done things that would most certainly haunt him for the rest of his life. For his team.

But that had been when things had changed. That

had been when his commanding officers had given him his nickname. The thin, white scar that disappeared into his beard became more pronounced.

"You're still on that team, Glennon. You have been since the day I met you," he said.

"Anthony..." She didn't know what to say to that. What *could* she say? Glennon backed toward the bed, the soft part of her knees hitting the mattress. This was a mistake. Had she known asking for Anthony's help would put him in this position, she never would've dialed his number.

She studied the mess around her. They were standing in the middle of a crime scene. She had a job to do. She hadn't come back to Anchorage to tear open past wounds, but she wasn't about to give him false hope, either. Notching her chin parallel to the floor, she stood. One step. Two. Debris parted as she closed the space between them. His masculine scent washed over her as she reached up, framing his strong jaw between her hands. "I...can't."

She'd promised herself not to get involved with any partner she'd been assigned. For the Military Police. With the army. First rule in rescue: keep emotional distance. She couldn't get involved, couldn't risk her emotions taking over a case. And she couldn't do personal relationships anymore. Not since...him. And not since her son had come along. Because a relationship didn't just involve her anymore. It would affect Hunter's life, too.

But Anthony tested that boundary as he stared down at her. She traced the small white scar that cut across the left side of his face with the pad of her thumb, one she'd never noticed before, hidden beneath his soft facial hair. Sliding his palms over the back of her hands, he leaned into her touch. He gave a single, quick nod. "I know."

Her hands slipped from his but she couldn't move—couldn't think—as he backed away. The outline of her engagement ring was still visible through his shirt. How had she not recognized it for what it was before now?

"We should go." He started walking toward the door, taking every ounce of heat from her body with him. "The marshal isn't going to wait around all day for us to ambush him."

"Anthony." She fisted her grip around the hem of her jacket to keep from reaching out for him. Seconds passed. Ten. Maybe more. What was she supposed to say? The ring, his confession… She hadn't been prepared for any of it. "I'm sorry. I wish I could—"

"Don't do that." Hand on the doorknob, he cocked his head over his shoulder. "You got exactly what you wanted, Glennon. And it didn't matter who you left behind in the process."

She schooled her expression as his words shot straight through her.

He wrenched open the door.

"I wasn't finished." Her voice turned to ice while

every cell in her body caught fire. "You might think you have me figured out, that I left because of some pathetic fear of commitment. But you're wrong." Her feet sank into the floor as though they'd been buried in cement. "What I was going to say was that I wish I could tell you the truth."

"What do you mean?" Anthony turned to her. The lines between his eyebrows deepened as the heavy door automatically closed behind him. His voice dropped, deep, dark and sexy, and a shiver slid through her. "What truth?"

How could he possibly still affect her like this? Like they hadn't been apart the last five years. Like her entire world hadn't flipped the second she'd set eyes on him. Like she was still the rookie in basic training who'd fallen head over heels for the Ranger she'd met during weapons training.

She bit the side of her tongue. She couldn't do it. Couldn't tell him. Because no matter how much Anthony deserved to know, she couldn't stand the possibility of him hating her more than he already did. She needed his help to find Bennett—plain and simple—and she couldn't risk him walking away.

Pressure built in her lungs the longer he stared at her, expecting answers. Only there was nothing simple about their situation, was there? "That I'm sorry for leaving the way I did. I shouldn't have disappeared while you were on tour. Doesn't change my reasons for leaving. But after I heard what happened to you in Afghanistan, I realized too late I should've done a lot of things differently."

Anthony didn't flinch. Not so much as a muscle-twitch. His pulse beat steadily at the base of his throat as he studied her, always in control. Always assessing. But he couldn't possibly know what she was hiding. He nodded. "You know you clench your fingers into a fist when you lie, right?"

"I do not." She glanced down at her hands. Uncurling her fingers, Glennon rubbed her palms down the sides of her thighs. She'd had that specific tell under control for years. What had changed? She raised her gaze to his. Hell. Didn't she already know the answer to that?

She cleared her throat. "I called in a few favors after I left. I know you spent two days in enemy territory alone, out of ammunition, out of provisions, and that the only way you made it back alive was by shooting your way out."

He closed in on her, fire, rage—everything he kept caged from her—bleeding to the surface of his tightly held control. Not to intimidate her but to get her attention, to let her know he wasn't about to back down.

She was forced to look up at him. Didn't he realize she hadn't been able to focus on anything but him the last two days? That it took every ounce of her remaining strength to keep her distance?

"I'm trained to read people, Glennon. That means

I can read you." He traced the length of her neck with his fingertips, catching her off guard. An explosion of need filled her. She held her breath.

Leveling those dark blue eyes with hers, he leaned in close. So close all she had to do was shift forward to meet his lips if she wanted to. "Just answer me about one thing. Honestly."

Her heart beat loud behind her ears.

"Is whatever you're hiding going to get us killed?" he asked.

She shook her head. "No."

"Then that's all I need to know." He slid his hand to the back of her neck and pulled her into him. Crushing her against him, Anthony kissed her with a punishing desire she'd never felt before. He surrounded her, controlled her, slid his mouth over hers as though he'd been waiting for this moment since the day she left.

And she let him.

She'd wanted—no, *needed*—this release, needed *him*, more than anything else at the moment. Forget Bennett. Forget the investigation. Forget she'd landed in the crosshairs of a sniper and could take another bullet at any moment. Right now, there was only Anthony. Her strong, reliable, loyal Ranger. If only for a few seconds, she'd give up control. She'd let the feelings she'd buried for the last five years take over. Her insides caught fire as she melted against him. Had it always been like this between them? So freeing? Roaring electricity shot up her spine. Hell, she was an idiot for kissing him back, but how long had it been since she'd trusted someone this completely?

His fingertips pressed into the back of her skull, refusing to let her budge as he swept his tongue past her lips. He worked to claim her from the inside and—right in the middle of her destroyed barracks, with her peers on the other side of the door—she didn't care. No hesitation.

Passion and familiarity spread through her as his full beard tickled the oversensitized skin along her jaw. The sensation only spurred her further. She kissed him back, kissed him with everything she had. Shoving years of loneliness, of pain and self-doubt into the near-forgotten connection between them, Glennon surrendered for the first time in years. To him. Always to him.

Anthony pulled back first and she swayed on her feet. His masculine scent drove through her system, determined to mark her from the inside. Staring down at her, he shifted on his feet, but kept her close. "I've wanted to do that since the moment I saw you in that abandoned house."

Abandoned house? She blinked to clear her head. Right. The investigation. Her partner.

Glennon maneuvered out of his grasp. His pupils grew smaller as she ran a hand through her hair. Air. She needed air. She'd gotten so lost in him, she'd completely forgotten why she'd called him in the first place. To find Bennett. Rolling her lips between her teeth, she bit down to get her head back in the game. It'd felt good to let go for those countless seconds, to give up her control for a moment, but it couldn't happen again. Not with him. Not with anyone.

Glennon moved to the door. "You're right. The marshal isn't going to wait around all day for us to interrogate him. Let's go."

Chapter Six

She'd lied to him.

While she'd claimed whatever she was hiding wouldn't ultimately get them killed, Anthony had read the distress in her expression. He slid his finger along the side of his Beretta as they waited outside the downtown office building. Civilian turf. Nothing to tie back to Glennon if this went south. According to the lieutenant general's administrative assistant, the marshal had a meeting scheduled here in ten minutes. Enough time to get some answers.

Glennon hadn't said a word since they'd left the barracks, but the uneven tension straining her jawline as she watched out the passenger-side window for their target revealed the truth: he shouldn't have kissed her.

Anthony wouldn't apologize. He wasn't sorry. But the silence that had filled the inside of the tinted SUV pressurized the air in his lungs. "Want to talk about it?"

"There's nothing to talk about." She kept her eyes on the side mirror. "You kissed me. I kissed you back. Won't happen again. The end."

He tapped the back of his head against his headrest, his grip light on the Beretta in his lap. As much as he wanted to believe she meant every word, he'd been part of that kiss, too. She'd surrendered to him. For those few brief moments she'd given up her tight control, had reverted to the woman he'd fallen in love with during her basic training. And damn, what he wouldn't give to feel that release again. To see her let go. "How can you be sure it won't happen again?"

"There's our target." Glennon sat forward in her seat, unholstering her service weapon as the marshal's nontactical vehicle pulled up to the underground parking garage of the building with two armed military escorts. She unlocked the door and shouldered her weight into it. "Let's go see if the marshal wants me dead."

Anthony was right behind her. His boots hit the asphalt, instincts on high alert. They'd lost the advantage of ambushing Lieutenant General Sykes under the cover of darkness, but he wasn't about to open fire in the middle of a public street, either. They had to be smart about this or risk involving Anchorage PD, the army and any other interested parties—the last thing Glennon wanted in this investigation.

She jogged across the street, gun at her side.

Anthony surveyed the area in case Sykes was

being watched. Tall, with a slight build, headed into his seventies with a full head of white hair and deep wrinkles, the marshal didn't scream suspected traitor, but Anthony wasn't taking any chances. Not with Glennon in the crosshairs. The rooftops were clear. No civilians took more of an interest in their movements than normal. So far, so good.

Glennon picked up the pace when the tail end of Sykes's vehicle cleared the entrance to the garage, but she pulled up short once she approached the corner. Back pressed against the wall, she closed her eyes for a split second then turned to Anthony. She locked on him, determined, controlled. One hundred percent the special agent he'd imagined she'd become. "If this goes sideways, we'll be court-martialed. You can still back out."

No. He couldn't.

"I've got your back." His pulse beat steadily in his chest. This was what he did for a living, what he'd been born to do. Adrenaline dumped into his blood. Primary objective: protect Glennon. If her interrogation with the marshal went south, he'd get her out of there. No matter what. Giving up wasn't in her personality, but her life was far more important than this investigation. He pulled back the slide on his weapon, ensuring he'd loaded a round into the chamber. He nodded once. "On your signal."

"Go." Glennon swung her Glock up as she rounded the corner.

A rush of icy air slammed into him as they descended into the darkness. His senses adjusted slowly. Glennon's outline was straight ahead of him. She moved with quick, sure movements toward Sykes's NTV parked in the second row at the back of the garage. No sign of the marshal or his armed escorts. Anthony listened for movement. The start of a car, footsteps—anything to give them an idea where their target had gone. He gripped the Berretta tighter.

Nothing. The garage was too quiet for this time of day.

As they neared the NTV, he caught sight of two bodies. Two soldiers. His instincts prickled a warning. Damn it. Sykes had known they were coming.

Anthony lunged for Glennon up ahead, wrapping his hand around her arm. He tugged her into him a split second before a bullet ripped through the darkness. Cement exploded to their left as a column absorbed the shot. Her breath slammed out of her chest and across his neck with the impact. Shuffling sounds echoed off the asphalt, but not long enough for Anthony to pin down their target's location. Her fingers gripped his Kevlar vest, keeping him pressed against her. His fight-or-flight instinct sharpened his senses. He sure as hell wouldn't take flight. The son of a bitch had taken a shot at her. Wouldn't happen again.

"You shouldn't have come here, Sergeant Chase,"

a deep, drawling accented voice called out. "You're in over your head."

Glennon's chin notched higher, her shoulders stiffening. She rolled off him. Follow the plan. She'd distract Sykes while Anthony closed in on the target. "Is that the same warning you gave Sergeant Spencer when he confronted you about your ties to Mascaro's operation?"

A low rumble of a laugh vibrated through the garage as Anthony maneuvered along the south wall of the garage, gun in hand. The marshal's voice barely reached him. "You have no idea what you're talking about, little girl. The operation you and your partner have been investigating is more than you can take on. Hell, it's more than the US Army can take on. Sergeant Spencer understood that."

The outline of a man about Sykes's height and build moved from around a white van thirty feet ahead. Toward Glennon's position.

Anthony focused on the four cars between him and the marshal. She could take care of herself, he had no doubt about that, but he picked up his pace all the same. He heel-toed it across the cement, ensuring he kept his weight evenly distributed so the lieutenant general wouldn't know what hit him. The muscles in his shoulders ached the longer he held the gun up, deprived of oxygen as he held his breath.

"Did you kill him?" Glennon's voice wavered.

Three cars between him and the target. Anthony

kept low and moved fast. Two cars. The scent of spicy aftershave clouded his head.

"I barely escaped with my life after Sergeant Spencer came looking for me." Sykes's outline sharpened as Anthony closed in. The marshal raised his weapon and took aim. A quick glance in Glennon's position revealed how close she'd gotten. Too close. And directly into Sykes's sights. "I won't make the same mistake with you, Sergeant."

Anthony pulled the trigger.

The bullet ripped through his target's shoulder, an almost identical wound to Glennon's. The marshal crumbled to the pavement, a rich groan filling the garage. But to Sykes's credit, he didn't scream.

Dim overhead lighting chased the shadows from Glennon's features as she moved in, weapon aimed at her commanding officer. Even with a bullet in his shoulder, Sykes was a highly trained military operative in his glory days. A threat.

Anthony kicked the marshal's gun across the pavement, out of reach. Metal scraped against asphalt as the weapon disappeared under a parked car a few spaces down.

"The mistake you made was assuming I'd come without backup." Glennon crouched low as the marshal clamped a hand over the hole in his shoulder.

Blood seeped from between the lieutenant general's fingers, but Sykes would live to tell his tale. As long as they got their answers. Someone had sent a professional shooter after Glennon, then another man to break into his cabin. Anthony wasn't leaving until he found out who would be on the wrong end of his weapon next time.

"Where is Sergeant Spencer?" Glennon's voice promised a not-too-happy ending for the marshal.

Anthony's phone vibrated in his pocket. One look at Captain Reise's email and the forwarded scene report from Glennon's barracks said they had the right guy. "Your fingerprints were all over Sergeant Chase's barracks." He nodded toward the marshal, but Glennon only had attention for her commanding officer. Not a hint of surprise on those beautiful, stone-like features. "He destroyed the files you gathered on Bennett and Sergeant Mascaro's operation. Should've been more careful, sir."

The marshal didn't respond. No surprise there. Trained operatives spent hundreds of hours counteracting interrogation tactics. Sykes wouldn't admit guilt, but the small twitch of his white beard gave way to another almost inaudible groan.

"Tell me where Sergeant Spencer is, and you might be able to call an ambulance in time," she said.

"You don't scare me, Sergeant Chase. You're not a killer." The marshal's chapped lips thinned into a smile. He checked back over his shoulder, toward Anthony. "As for the company you keep, that's a different story."

Glennon blinked. "You don't know anything about us."

"Oh, I know plenty, darlin'." A thick Texan accent bubbled to the surface. Sweat across Sykes's forehead reflected the dim overhead lighting. Blood loss tended to have that effect—it drained color from the face, forced the hands to shake. "I know you're from Anchorage. That your daddy walked out on you and your mama at a young age. That you were engaged to Sergeant Major Harris here before you transferred to the Quantico office. And that you, my dear, are not prepared for what's about to happen."

"You killed your escort," she said. "Why?"

Anthony searched the garage. They weren't getting anywhere with this guy. The marshal wouldn't tell them anything about her missing partner. He caught sight of the elevators at the north end of the building, the panel above the doors counting down. Level three. Level two. The hairs on the back of his neck stood on end. "Glennon."

"And I know your secret," Lieutenant General Sykes said. "The one you've been keeping from the army and your bodyguard here."

Anthony homed in on the marshal.

Straightening, Glennon lowered the Glock to her side. If the garage hadn't been so dark, Anthony would've sworn the blood had drained from her face. Her gun hand shook briefly, but she stilled so fast, he could've been mistaken. "You're lying."

Level one.

"Glennon, he's baiting you so he can stall." Anthony maneuvered around the marshal. Someone was about to step off that elevator and, from their current position fewer than fifty feet from the doors, blow their entire operation. "We've got to get out of here."

Bright red lines across the elevator's electric panel said they were out of time.

"Your partner had a secret, too, Sergeant Chase." The lines around Sykes's eyes deepened—to counteract the pain in his shoulder, most likely. "Don't suppose the fact Sergeant Spencer is a lieutenant in Nicholas Mascaro's operation is the reason he's gone missing, do you?"

The elevator doors parted.

HER WORLD SLOWED.

Anthony raised his weapon in her peripheral vision. Thumping vibrations shot through her as sparks exploded off two cars nearby, but Glennon couldn't move. It wasn't possible. The marshal was lying. Bennett wouldn't have gotten himself involved with a criminal organization. Everything they'd done the last six months had been to bring down Mascaro's operation... He wasn't a lieutenant.

"Glennon!" Anthony shoved her down. "Get out of here!"

The dimly lit garage blurred as she hit the ground. Reality caught up as Lieutenant General Sykes army-crawled away from her. Bullets ricocheted off the vehicle at her back, and she shook her head clear. The Glock remained heavy in her grip as she lunged. Catching his arm with one hand, Glennon ripped her commanding officer from the asphalt and ran. Sykes wasn't going anywhere. Not until she had what she came for.

Anthony fired two shots—three—as he followed close on her heels. "Go, go, go!"

Who the hell was shooting at them?

She pumped her legs hard, dragging the marshal behind her with everything she had. The bullet in his shoulder slowed them down, but she wasn't about to leave him behind. He jerked forward—trying to rip away—but Glennon kept a tight hold on his arm.

They dove behind a white commercial van at the back of the garage. The rhythmic firing of automatic gunfire echoed loudly in her ears. The van would give them enough cover for the next few minutes, but they couldn't afford to be pinned down much longer. Every second she wasted trying to get answers out of Sykes limited her and Anthony's chance of escape.

She fought to catch her breath, turning on her commanding officer. She fisted his three-star-decorated uniform and wrenched him toward her. Asphalt bit into her knees with his added weight. "You're involved in Mascaro's operation. Tell me about Bennett. Now."

Something wet and sticky dripped down her T-shirt.

"Seems like we're both running out of time, Sergeant Chase." The marshal's coffee-brown eyes glassed over.

Blood. He'd been shot in the chest. No, no, no, no. "Come on. Stay with me, Marshal. Tell me where my partner is."

"We're pinned down." Maneuvering around the van, Anthony crouched low and switched his magazine for a fresh reload.

Relief flooded through her, but didn't last long. He'd get them out of here. Whatever it took, she believed in him. But the provost marshal general was losing blood fast and the chances of getting information out of him were quickly dwindling. Hell burned in Anthony's cold blue eyes, locked on Sykes, and a shiver chased down her spine. This had been exactly why she'd come to him for help.

Focusing on the blood spreading across the asphalt, Anthony shook his head. "He took a bullet to his left lung. He'll suffocate before we have a chance to even move him." His voice was flat.

"That's not good enough." The gunfire pounded through her head, never ceasing. How were they going to get out of here? "Please—" she leveraged both palms against Sykes's wound to stop the bleeding, in vain "—tell me about Sergeant Spencer. What happened to him? Where can I find him?"

"Mascaro…paid me…will kill… Sergeant Spen—"

Blood stained the corners of Lieutenant General Sykes's mouth as he sagged back against the pavement. A rough exhale escaped him as the life drained from his aged features.

"No. You're not allowed to die on me! Tell me where Bennett is." Glennon leveraged her weight and pumped eight quick pulses to get his heart started. Counting another eight, she barely registered the strong grip trying to pull her back. Wrenching out of Anthony's hold, she slid her blood-covered fingertips to her commanding officer's neck. No pulse. Frustration climbed up her throat.

The marshal stared at the ceiling, unmoving.

He was dead. And any information he'd had about recovering Bennett had died with him.

"Glennon, we need to get out of here!" Anthony's voice barely registered over the gunfire that seemed so much louder than a few minutes ago. Strong hands ripped her from beside the marshal's body and thrust her toward the back of the van.

"The only way we're getting out of here is through the main entrance." Another round of bullets ricocheted off the vehicle. Three shots? Four? Glennon couldn't think. Her best chance of putting an end to this investigation had just bled out on the asphalt six feet away. Anthony unloaded the rest of his magazine at the shooters then took cover once again to switch weapons. "We need a plan here, sweetheart."

Blood coated her palms, but she gripped her Glock

hard nonetheless. A dull ringing filled her ears. Glennon shook the last few minutes of the lieutenant general's life from her memory. Sykes might've held the answers to her investigation, but she wasn't giving up. It wasn't in her personality. Dead or alive, she'd find Bennett and put an end to this nightmare. Even if she had to break a few of the very laws she'd upheld to do it.

She turned on Anthony. This wasn't over. "Mascaro's operatives want me." She counted the rounds left in her magazine and slammed it back into her weapon. "They're going to have to come get me."

"You hired me to protect you." Anthony took position at the corner of the van. Locking his eyes on her, he resurrected heated flashes of the gut-wrenching kiss they'd shared in her barracks. When he'd kissed her, she'd been lost. His fingers had threaded up the back of her neck and into her hair, and the rest of the world had fallen away for the briefest of moments. The scar disappearing into his full beard combined with tanned, weathered skin had turned him rough, but the way he'd held her, the way he'd touched her, revealed just how much he cared. He'd get them out of here. He'd take care of her. "And I'll be damned if I let you get yourself killed."

She swayed toward him. She nodded to focus. She couldn't think about that right now, couldn't think about him. Whoever these guys were—whoever had sent them—they weren't interested in talking. Professionals only wanted one thing: the target. Glennon glanced at her former commanding officer. If there were casualties in the process, that didn't matter. She'd get her answers one way or another. "I want to know what the marshal meant about Bennett being part of Mascaro's operation. I'll take the shooter on the left. You take the right. We need these guys alive."

"You got it, sweetheart." He rounded the van, weapon aimed, and fired.

Glennon followed close behind, taking the low ground. The two shooters had taken position across the aisle, each using a vehicle for cover. Gripping her Glock in both hands, she dropped to one knee and pulled the trigger. The gun kicked back in her hand, but she barely registered the pain in her shoulder this time around. Adrenaline pumped into her veins, focusing her senses on the single shooter to her left.

Kevlar and a bulletproof face mask absorbed her direct hits. Damn it. These two had come in full tactical gear. Army-level gear. She couldn't get a read on the man behind the lieutenant general's NTV. Had the shooters come on orders from Staff Sergeant Mascaro himself? Or had they been waiting to ambush the marshal? She redirected her aim, the air in her lungs pressurizing the longer their targets stayed upright. Only one way to find out.

Sinking to the pavement, Glennon flattened herself against the asphalt. Ice worked through her veins. Two shots was all it took to sweep the shooter's legs out from under him. He hit the hood of the NTV face-first and collapsed, dropping his weapon in the process. A deep groan hit her ears as she pushed to her feet.

Anthony closed in on his own target. The second shooter clamped down tight on a bullet wound that had skimmed his neck with one hand, but kept firing with the other. The gun clicked empty as Anthony charged. He slammed the shooter into the pavement, disappearing behind the car.

Heart in her throat, Glennon waited. One breath. Two. Shuffling teased her ears, but not from the shooter she'd taken down. Her jaw hardened. She gripped her gun tight. If one of those bullets had gotten through his gear... No. She couldn't think like that. Anthony was a Ranger. He'd taken plenty of hits over the years and delivered thousands more. Even with all those battle scars, he was the strongest, most loyal man she'd ever known. With calculated, slow steps, Glennon edged around the front of the vehicle.

Anthony wrenched the shooter to his feet, unbalanced.

"Damn it, don't do that to me again." She ran a hand through her hair. Sweat coated her palm. She wiped it down her pants, the tension pulling her shoulders tight then releasing in small increments. She breathed a bit easier. He was okay.

Until she noticed the dark, wet stain of blood spreading across the front of his thigh.

Anthony swayed on his feet, his eyelids heavy.

"You've been hit." The garage blurred in her peripheral vision as her blood pressure skyrocketed. Color drained from his face and Glennon rushed forward, ready to catch him if he collapsed.

Stinging pain spread across her skull as she was ripped back into a wall of Kevlar. "You're not going anywhere."

She twisted against her attacker's grip on her hair, hoping to plant her knee straight in his groin… But the hot metal of a gun barrel pressed to her forehead froze her to the spot. Deep brown eyes stared back at her but she couldn't make out any other features beneath his bulletproof face mask. He swung her around again, bracing her back to his vested chest as his free hand gripped her throat. A single glance at the back of the vehicle where she'd thought she'd taken out the first shooter said it all. She'd been played. He hadn't been injured, hadn't even been knocked unconscious.

"Sergeant Chase—" his deep voice echoed from under the mask "—I've been waiting to get my hands on you."

Chapter Seven

Anthony's grip tightened around the unconscious shooter in his grasp while the second pointed a gun at Glennon's head. Pain splintered his racing thoughts. He couldn't see her face, but the deep reserve of rage he'd buried over the years took control all the same. It had started with losing every member of his team behind enemy lines and it had ended when Glennon had walked out the door. He wasn't about to lose another teammate. He wasn't about to lose her.

"Break a single hair on her head and it'll be the last mistake you ever make," he said.

Sweat beaded under his jawline, his vision blurring for a split second. His heart jolted in his chest. Fury built in him, a deadly rage that wouldn't be controlled. He let the bastard's partner collapse, the body hitting the pavement hard with fifty-plus pounds of gear. His fingers curled into his palm, tingling with the urge to wrap his hands around his Beretta. Or the bastard's throat. He wasn't picky. If it came right down to it, he'd beat the life out of any man who dared threaten her. No matter how much blood he lost. Which, by looking at the puddle under his left boot, had been quite a bit.

"Big words coming from a man bleeding out in the middle of a parking garage." The shooter's voice lacked any distinct accent, his face hidden beneath layers of gear. Anthony could barely make out anything clearly other than brown—almost black—eyes. Six feet, about two hundred pounds of pure muscle. No visible tattoos or birthmarks. The only way they'd get a clue to this guy's ID and whoever had hired him would be with an autopsy. And as the seconds passed, Anthony was becoming more comfortable with that route.

The shooter was playing it safe, positioning Glennon fully in front of him, using her as a shield as he moved the gun barrel to her temple. "What do you think, Sergeant Chase?" He pressed his face mask against her ear and the muscles down Anthony's spine jerked. "Should I finish him off now or let him go out the hard way? My orders never said anything about bringing *him* back alive. I was only paid to get intel out of you. By whatever means necessary."

Sergeant Chase. Orders. The way the guy talked spoke volumes. They were dealing with soldiers. Nothing he hadn't handled before, but the bullet in his thigh might be a problem. He had to stay conscious. Keep her alive. With his veiled admission to needing to bring Glennon back alive, the shooter had given away more intel than he'd probably meant to. The bastard had been sent by Mascaro. And with Lieutenant General Sykes's involvement, they now had proof—her and Bennett's investigation for the army had been compromised after all.

"What makes you think he's going to let you walk out of this alive?" she asked the shooter. Glennon nodded to Anthony, her expression steady. Not an ounce of fear darkened those mesmerizing green eyes, but he read her uncertainty in the way her knuckles whitened as she held on to the shooter's wrist at her throat. She swallowed hard.

"Should we test that theory?" The shooter pressed the barrel of the gun harder into her temple, throwing Glennon off balance. "If I'm not walking out of here alive, neither are you."

Not going to happen.

Rage exploded from behind Anthony's rib cage and spread fast. The edges of his vision darkened, putting the bastard in the middle of his own personal crosshairs. Adrenaline dimmed the pain in his leg as he rushed forward. Screw the Beretta. He'd tear this SOB apart with his bare hands.

Understanding exactly what he intended to do, Glennon twisted and threw her elbow back into the shooter's face mask. Her captor dropped his hold from her throat, giving her an out. Anthony closed the distance between him and the shooter as she dove for the ground.

"She's not going anywhere with you." Fisting the Kevlar vest in his grasp, Anthony ripped the face mask and underlying ski mask from the shooter's head and tossed them at the nearest car door. The vehicle's alarm and flashing headlights kept rhythm with his racing heartbeat. He pulled back his arm, ready to end this once and for all. For Glennon.

Black hair and tanned skin were all he registered as a fist slammed into the right side of his face. The world tilted on its axis, but Anthony refused to let go of the man in his grip. Another hit landed home and he collapsed to one knee. Pavement cut into him. Copper and salt filled his mouth as the wound in his leg bled faster. But the pain—the dizziness—was nothing compared to what he'd endured for his country.

"Come on now, Ranger," the shooter said. "I've read your file. Give me a challenge."

Anthony spat salty blood onto the asphalt. This guy wanted a fight? All right. He'd give him everything he had. He straightened, but with the amount of blood pooling on the asphalt, quickly sank. He caught sight of Glennon reaching for her weapon a split second before the shooter planted his boot in the middle of her back.

A small gasp wheezed from her mouth.

"Don't worry, Sergeant Chase. I haven't forgotten

about you." The bastard kicked her gun underneath the nearest car then fell to one knee beside her rib cage as he lowered his voice. Blood from the raw wound along his neck dripped onto her flawless features. "Before this is over, you're going to give me what I want or die in the process."

A growl exploded from his chest as Anthony came up swinging. His fist connected with the shooter's bullet wound—shocking his opponent—but the guy wouldn't stop there. He lost the Kevlar, the protective gear that was only weighing him down.

Sweat slid underneath the collar of Anthony's shirt as Glennon scrambled for her weapon. "Take care of him." He nodded at the first shooter who still lay unconscious at the back of the car. "I've got this."

She disappeared behind the car, blood smeared across her expression.

His attacker charged. Catching the bastard at the neck and waistband, Anthony flipped him and slammed him into the pavement. The smell of cigarettes drifted up from the shooter's clothing as he landed a boot in the center of Anthony's chest. Anthony staggered back, but went in for another strike. The shooter rolled off the pavement, hands up, and blocked the hit. Legs staggered, knees bent, shoulders squared, elbows in. This guy was definitely military. Green Beret, if Anthony had to guess. And the only way to take down a Green Beret was death.

"There's the Ranger I've heard so much about."

The shooter pulled a blade from his ankle. "Show me what you've got."

Combatives training took control. Anthony wrapped his fingers around the guy's wrist and pulled him closer. Rotating the blade away and up, he drove his elbow into the shooter's twisted arm. The crunch of bone breaking quaked down his spine as the clash of steel and asphalt echoed throughout the garage. His knuckles met his assailant's jawbone and he quickly followed through with his elbow to the same spot.

The guy fell hard. A deep growl filled the silence. "That's more like it."

A combination of sweat and blood loss blurred Anthony's vision. He swayed on his feet. He didn't have long before he blacked out. Fisting the bastard's shirtfront, he wrenched the Green Beret to his feet. Pain surged through his thigh with the additional weight. "You tell Nicholas Mascaro as long as I'm around, Glennon Chase is off-limits. Understand?"

Swelling consumed one deep brown eye, an uneven smile curling the shooter's mouth. "You can't protect her forever, Ranger. Even if you kill me now, they'll send someone to take my place." A deep rumble of a laugh worked up the SOB's throat. "One way or another, your woman and her partner are dead. You're just extending the date they'll carve on their gravestones."

His woman. Anthony's grip tightened.

Overhead lighting glinted off a flash of metal in his peripheral vision. But he wasn't fast enough. The Green Beret swung another small blade fast, and it landed home. The breath rushed from Anthony's lungs, agony ripping through him. He'd taken bullets, sustained stab wounds. None had taken him out of commission before, but he doubled forward now. Glennon's engagement ring fell from under his shirt collar. The edges of his vision darkened.

"No!" Her shadowed outline rushed toward him. "Anthony!"

"Don't worry, Sergeant Major Harris." The blade slid from between his ribs as a strong grip squeezed his shoulder. The shooter set his mouth against Anthony's ear. "I'm going to take real good care of her."

Two distinct gunshots exploded. From a Glock. Glennon's service weapon? He couldn't be sure. The shooter jerked against him but didn't go down, spinning toward the source. Anthony shook his head to clear the fuzziness closing in fast, but strength drained from his muscles every second he wasted trying to get his bearings.

The grip on his shoulder vanished. He couldn't breathe. Couldn't think. Where was she? He blinked to restart his system. Blood and sweat drenched his clothing. He had to get up. Had to get Glennon out of here. Fisting his hands, Anthony shoved to his feet. He'd lost a lot of blood, but he had enough left pumping through his veins to finish this.

The shooter closed in on her. Her gun clicked empty and she took two steps back, that beautiful green gaze searching for something—anything—to fight back with. She widened her stance, fists up. Blocking the first hit, Glennon knocked the Green Beret's weapon from his hand but wasn't fast enough to counter the second hit. His fingers wrapped around her neck as he sandwiched her between his body and the hood of the nearest car. She bowed against the metal, one hand on his wrist, another hitting her attacker as hard as she could—but the hit barely fazed him. He was too strong.

"Let her go." Every cell in Anthony's body propelled him forward. No thought. Only Glennon. In a split second he secured the shooter's head between both hands and wrenched as hard as he could. The body collapsed to the asphalt. He stared down at the single brown eye that hadn't swollen shut from the fight, his breath sawing in and out of his lungs.

It was over. For now. He sank his weight into his uninjured leg, clamping a hand over the stab wound in his side.

"On second thought, I'll tell Staff Sergeant Mascaro myself," he said.

THE GRIM REAPER had arrived. And her attacker had most certainly pissed him off.

Glennon rubbed at her throat, swallowing back the last twenty minutes. She leveraged her weight against the hood of the car to keep from collapsing. Bodies littered the ground. The marshal's escorts, the marshal himself, the two shooters sent to retrieve her. So much blood. What the hell had Bennett gotten himself into?

"Anthony," she said.

His name left her lips as a whisper. That was all she could manage right now. She locked her attention on the engagement ring around his neck, the one smeared with crusted blood. She closed the distance between them slowly but he never focused on her. A pool of dark liquid collected under his left boot. Bullet to the thigh. Stab wound to the rib cage. Had there been more damage? Framing her fingers along his jawline, she forced him to look her in the eye. "Talk to me."

Sirens reached her ears. She glanced toward the garage entrance. Ambushing the marshal, capturing one of the shooters in the hope of doing their own interrogation…this whole thing had been a mistake. And all to find a missing partner who might be involved in the very operation she'd been trying to bring to justice. She had to get Anthony out of there before local police showed up. "Okay, come on."

Glennon stopped cold. Guns. Where were their guns? Hell, she couldn't leave them behind. Their prints would put them in the center of a manhunt once Anchorage PD collected them as evidence. And the army would follow. She couldn't have her name on those reports. Couldn't put her son at risk.

Swinging Anthony's arm over her shoulders, she maneuvered him against the side of the nearest car. And she couldn't do that to Anthony. Not after everything he'd done for her the past two days. Her stress response drained from her system as she crawled beneath both parked cars. One Beretta, one Glock.

Anthony pushed away from the vehicle, trying to stand. How he was still conscious, she had no idea, but she couldn't do this by herself.

The sirens grew louder. She didn't have time to collect bullet casings, and there were far too many scattered across the entire garage for her to get them all. Exhaustion dragged her down as she hefted Anthony into her side again. His solid weight unbalanced her. "You can do this, baby. I'm going to get you help. We just have to get to the SUV."

Baby? Heat crawled into her cheeks. Where the hell had that come from? Glennon shoved the thought to the back of her mind. She had more important things to worry about right now. And, with any luck, he wouldn't remember any of this later.

He mumbled something unintelligible as she hauled him up the garage entrance ramp. Sunlight blinded her for a split second. She guarded her eyes against the blazing sun, but quickly leveraged her hand into his chest to hold Anthony upright as his legs started giving out. He'd parked the SUV a little over a block away on the other side of the street. They would make it. She had to believe that. Her throat ached. "Come on. You got this."

Head down, she dragged him across the road. Pressure of civilian stares as they passed built in her chest. Two people, both covered in blood, walking down the street. Nothing to be alarmed about. The first patrol car swung around the corner at the end of the block and she rammed herself into Anthony's un-injured side to take cover behind a car parked along the road. The street was about to be shut down and when Anchorage PD identified the bodies, the army would take over. They had to move. Her previous experience with local PD told her they had about three minutes. Another patrol car rounded the block, lights and sirens blaring. Make that one minute. Shoving her hands in his cargo pants' pockets, she searched for the SUV's keys. "Don't get any bright ideas. I'm trying to save your life."

"At least take me to dinner first." His words slurred, his eyes heavy. Was he even coherent?

"It's a date." A smile pulled at one edge of her mouth as her fingers closed around the key fob. Even in life-or-death situations, he could make her laugh. That'd been one of the reasons she'd fallen in love with him all those years ago. His unyielding determination to put her first. No matter how hard the situation. The smile vanished. Had she ever really fallen out of love? She liked to think she hadn't been holding on to him all this time, but after what he'd done back in that garage for her, after he'd saved her life... No. Now wasn't the time.

Glennon pressed the button to start the SUV. "But let's make sure you don't bleed out on the sidewalk first."

She hauled the passenger-side door open.

The door's side mirror exploded. She flinched away, gripping Anthony's shoulder and shoving him inside the vehicle. "Get down!"

Return fire from at least three police officers reached her ears, but didn't stop another bullet from whizzing past her head. Heart trying to pump out of her chest, she reached for one of the many guns Anthony had installed inside the SUV and took position at the back quarter panel.

The second shooter, the one she'd zip-tied after Anthony had knocked him unconscious, fired back at police. One officer went down. Then another. The shooter fell as a bullet hit his Kevlar dead center from the third, but was already straightening. What the hell were these guys made of? Steel? He raised his gun, and Glennon pulled back. A third shot ricocheted off the SUV's bumper. One glance in the shattered side mirror revealed Anthony had passed out. Too much blood loss. "Damn it."

Should she try to take down the shooter with orders to capture her, or get Anthony to the hospital?

Her thumb released the gun's safety mechanism.

No question. She had to get him out of here. And a quick check over her shoulder said she didn't have much time. The shooter was closing in on them. Fast.

She dove into the back seat, climbing behind the steering wheel as fast as she could. Reaching for Anthony's seat belt, she strapped him in but didn't bother with her own as the back window shattered. Apparently this Blackhawk vehicle's windows weren't bulletproof.

She started the engine, ducked down in the driver's seat, hauled the vehicle into Drive and slammed on the accelerator. The SUV launched away from the scene. In the rearview mirror, she saw the shooter climb into a waiting car.

"I thought you said this thing was bulletproof." Her breathing hitched as the SUV fishtailed at the end of the block. She couldn't go straight to the hospital. Not with a psychopath who was willing to take down civilians right behind them. Couldn't lead him to Blackhawk Security. Although a welcoming party wasn't a bad idea… No. She couldn't risk anyone else taking a bullet for her or becoming Nicholas Mascaro's next target. The uneven thump of her heart beat hard behind her ears. Glennon tapped her palm against the steering wheel. "Anthony, come on. Stay with me."

He'd know what to do. But one look at his colorless, slackened features said he wouldn't be waking up anytime soon. They had nowhere to go. And they'd run out of time.

Daytime headlights blazed directly behind the SUV as she accelerated onto Seward Highway. Snow-crusted mountains and dried pine trees hugged one side of the road. Turnagain Arm waterway was on the other as they sped out of the city. Hints of pink and orange, reflected on the icy water, were already turning the sky to fire. She could lose the shooter once the sun went down, but her instincts said they didn't have that long.

"We're going to get you help." She didn't have any other choice. She'd have to try to escape them now. At least long enough to get Anthony stable. Wrapping her fingers around his lifeless hand in his lap, she squeezed. Her lower eyelids stung. "Hang on for a little bit longer. Please."

She couldn't lose him. Not now. There hadn't been a chance to tell him everything. About why she'd left, how often she regretted her decision, how many times she'd thought about picking up that phone. But it was more than that. He was Anthony. Her first love, her biggest supporter, the first glimpse of her future, the man who, in the past forty-eight hours, had dedicated himself to her survival. The man she'd missed. The man who altered her breathing every time he touched her...

Glennon took a deep, calming breath. She'd get

him out of this one way or another. She owed him that much.

Slush and chunks of ice kicked up around the vehicle, the SUV's tires spinning out as she turned around one smooth corner of highway. She'd learned to drive in Anchorage winters as a teenager. She could handle it.

Glancing in the rearview mirror, she kept tabs on the shooter's vehicle as it closed the distance between them. Freezing Alaskan air worked its way inside through the webbed back window as the sound of a growling engine reached her ears from behind. Through the shooter's windshield, she spotted the gun in his hand as he rolled down his window. She forced her attention back to the road ahead. Just a bit farther.

Two shots echoed off the cliffs.

She ducked lower in her seat, knuckles white on the steering wheel. They were going to make it. No matter what. She'd get Anthony the help he needed. Another glance in the rearview mirror—

A forty-ton Mack truck pulled onto the highway directly in front of her.

The breath rushed out of her. Glennon hit the brakes, tires locking as she pressed her spine into the seat. She gripped the steering wheel with both hands and swerved to avoid the truck, throwing herself into Anthony's shoulder.

The front end of the SUV missed the truck by

mere inches as she cut across the highway and through a wooden guardrail. Weeds and mud covered the windshield as she slammed on the brakes again. The tires slipped on the thick ice clinging to Turnagain Arm's shoreline. They were going too fast. The lip of the shore catapulted the SUV into the air and they dove headfirst. Gravity crushed her into her seat as she reached for Anthony. "I've got you. Just hang—"

Chapter Eight

The collision of metal meeting ice thrust Anthony forward in his seat. The seat belt cut into his chest as crystal-clear water rushed across the windshield. His head slammed back into the passenger seat. Vision blurred, he blinked to clear his head as pain rushed through his system. The front of the SUV pitched engine-first into deep water, a steady horizon of water climbing up the length of the windshield. His heels automatically dug against the floor. They were going under.

Deadly calm slid over him. He'd survived worse. And under fire. But Glennon...damn it. Where was Glennon?

He caught sight of her slumped against the steering wheel, her face angled away from him. She hadn't buckled her seat belt.

"Glennon." His throat threatened to close with his next breath. Releasing his seat belt, Anthony dove for her as freezing Alaskan water rushed across his boots. They had two minutes, maybe three, before the interior of the SUV would be submerged completely. He pulled her from the steering wheel. Her head snapped back, but no response. A thin line of blood highlighted the angles of her features as it ran under her shirt. He brushed a strand of hair from her wound as water climbed up his shins. "Open your eyes, sweetheart."

Nothing. Color had drained from her normally flawless skin but a thready pulse beat against his fingers. He had to get her out. At these temperatures, and with the water soaking through their clothing, hypothermia would set in a lot faster than normal.

"Okay." He ducked to see through the now-broken rear windshield. The SUV had landed approximately twenty feet from shore. They didn't have any other choice. "We're going to have to swim for it."

After that? He'd have to go for the survival supplies Blackhawk Security operatives were required to carry in their vehicles. And hope the lake didn't swallow them first. Water rose up his thighs, gushing into the bullet wound in the thickest part of his muscle. Pain zinged through him.

Anthony hauled her to him. His instincts screamed for him to get Glennon out of the vehicle—*now*—but they couldn't swim for the shore yet. Not until the lake had engulfed them completely.

"Stay with me, sweetheart." Seconds stretched into minutes. The last bit of daylight through the front windshield vanished. Ten more seconds. The water kept rising along the side windows. Five. He secured her against his side with one arm and reached for the door handle with his free hand. Ice pumped through his veins from the waist down. Setting his lips against her ear, he closed his eyes for a split second. "Stay with me, sweetheart. I'll get you out of here."

And he always kept his promises.

The SUV had sunk low enough that the driver's-side door was completely submerged. He used every ounce of his remaining strength against the door as his side of the SUV tipped toward the lake floor. A scream ripped up his throat as pain and thousands of pounds of water fought against him. Water no longer seeped through the floor into the vehicle's interior but rushed to fill the unoccupied space. No time to think. He filled his lungs with her rosy scent. And dove into the ice-cold depths.

Chunks of ice and thick weeds clouded his vision as he pulled Glennon from the SUV. Pressure built through his system. He'd get her to the shore. No matter what.

Twenty feet. That was all they had. Twenty feet until she was safe.

His muscles burned. Below-freezing temperatures slowed his movements. Every cell in his body screamed for release. Sunlight broke through the blackness and he kicked with everything he had toward it. Thin strands of blood floated ahead of him, almost racing him to the surface. Whether from his wounds or Glennon's, he didn't know. Did it matter?

His pulse pounded loud in his ears but slowed the more he struggled to the surface. Air pressurized in his lungs. His system was using oxygen reserves faster than he'd expected. He'd lost too much blood. He couldn't keep up this pace. He estimated five more feet until they broke through the surface. He blinked against the exhaustion weighing him down. With every push forward, both Glennon and his wounds pulled him down. At his current rate, they wouldn't have to worry about hypothermia. They'd both drown before it had a chance to take over.

No.

He wouldn't give up that easily. He'd failed his teammates once. He wouldn't fail her.

Bubbles rushed from his mouth and nose as he kicked harder. Two feet. One. Anthony broke through the surface first, shattered pieces of ice scratching against his neck as he hauled Glennon above water. His lungs seized. He fought for air but couldn't seem to get enough. His body's defenses were already succumbing to the low temperatures. Soon his heart rate would drop so low, he wouldn't be able to function. Then his organs would start shutting down.

And Glennon…she shook in his hold. Good. Her body was still trying to warm itself, but the dark tint of blue to her lips said she wasn't getting enough oxygen. He hugged her into his side but his body heat had dropped too low to do her any good.

Damn it. Focus. Get her to the shore. Get the water out of her lungs. "I've…got you…sweetheart. Almost…there."

Reaching for the closest grouping of weeds, he pulled them closer to the shoreline. Numbness worked through his fingers and up his arms. He had mere minutes. Three. Maybe four. He couldn't breathe. Couldn't think. Gurgling sounds reached his ears. The lake had consumed the SUV. And their supplies had gone down with it.

His boots hit land. Anthony dragged Glennon through the remaining wall of weeds and onto the snow-covered rocks. Setting her head against the ground, he lowered his ear to her mouth. She wasn't breathing. Her pulse beat unevenly against his fingers. Panic flooded through him. Covering her mouth with his, he plugged her nose and pushed air into her lungs. He found the spot over her breastbone and put all his strength into forcing the water from her lungs. The fuzziness surrounding his thoughts cleared but the numbness in his extremities would take a hell of a lot longer to shake. "Come on, baby."

Darkness circled the edges of his vision, but he wouldn't stop. Not until she opened her eyes.

She jerked beneath him with each compression, her skin pale. But still no response.

"Open your eyes, damn it." His control shattered.

Precious air his organs needed rushed from his lungs. He bit the inside of his mouth to keep from screaming. He'd already lost too many people in his life. His parents when he was nineteen. His Ranger team in Afghanistan. Her.

He hadn't thought about the future since Glennon had walked out on him all those years ago, but now…that future included Glennon. His Glennon. She wasn't walking away from him. Not again. And not like this. "Glennon, breathe!"

Water sputtered from between her lips as she coughed. Her chest contracted beneath his hands as he turned her onto her side. She scratched at the rocks beside her.

"That's it, sweetheart. Just breathe." The pressure that had built in his chest released. Anthony rubbed small circles into her back, struggling to stay conscious. He blinked against the wave of dizziness gripping him from head to toe. Spots of red stained the snow on his left side. His stab wound… His fingers closed around her Kevlar vest in a last attempt to stay upright. "I've…got you."

Anthony collapsed. His head hit the rocks, the lake's horizon at the wrong angle. Glennon didn't move, her expression peaceful but full of color. She'd survived. That was all that mattered. He'd done his job. She was safe. Ringing filled his ears. "Glennon…"

The growl of an engine echoed off the nearby

mountain. A car door slammed. Footsteps crunched through the thin crust of snow from behind, but he couldn't move. They'd been run off the road, he remembered now. He'd passed out from blood loss, but the shooter, the one who'd shot at them as they fled down the highway, must've survived. His hand ignored his brain's commands to reach for the gun strapped to his thigh. Chances the weapon would fire after taking a swim in below-freezing water were low. But if the bastard had come to finish the job, Anthony would fight until the end.

"You know, we were ordered to bring Sergeant Chase back alive, but it looks like the problem has taken care of itself." The shooter he'd knocked unconscious stood above him. He pulled his mask over his head, green eyes and facial scars twisting with a thin smile. Dog tags swung from around the man's neck. Planting a steel-toed tactical boot across Anthony's chest, he pointed the barrel of a Smith & Wesson handgun center-mass. "As for you, you're just the icing on the cake."

The onset of hypothermia had already started shutting down Anthony's system. He fought against the weight pressing him into the ground. He'd lost too much blood. He focused on the slow rise and fall of Glennon's chest. He'd lost everything. "Stay away from her—"

Three gunshots exploded across the shore.

The shooter hit the ground, unmoving. Another

set of footsteps broke through the thin layer of ice clinging to the rocks around them. Stepping into the stream of sunlight, gun in hand, the figure crouched beside Anthony but didn't move to take another shot. Recognition flared.

"I warned her to back off." Sharp, angled features blurred in Anthony's vision as darkness closed in. Gravel coated the soldier's voice, exactly as Anthony remembered from the morning the intruder had broken into the cabin. The soldier holstered his weapon then reached for Anthony. "She should've listened."

"You're both lucky to be alive," an unfamiliar female voice said.

Glennon cracked her eyelids. Fluorescent lighting blinded her for a split second as she blinked to adjust. The machines a few feet away registered her stats. The last memories before they'd gone into the lake flashed across her mind. She homed in on the woman seated near the door and licked the dryness from her lips. Elizabeth Dawson. Blackhawk's network security expert. Her throat burned. Exhaustion pulled at her, but she forced herself to focus.

"How did I get here?" Five simple words. So much energy to get them out. She rubbed at her throat and blinked against the onslaught of fluorescent lighting. What the hell had happened on that highway? How had she gotten to the hospital? The last thing she remembered was screaming Anthony's name before they'd gone into the lake.

Didn't matter. She'd survived. And if the army had discovered she had a son as the marshal had said, then Mascaro's operatives undoubtedly knew about him, too. She had to get out of here. She had to see Hunter.

"An anonymous Good Samaritan saw the whole thing," Elizabeth said. "He drove you both to the hospital himself. Said Anthony pulled you out of the SUV and onto the shore."

Glennon pushed back against the bed to sit up. Pain shot through her shoulder and she locked her jaw to keep a moan at bay. How long did it take for a bullet wound to heal anyway?

"Where is Anthony?" Her words were thick, heavy.

"Resting. He'll live. Sullivan's with him now." Amusement played across Elizabeth's mouth as she studied Glennon from her position. The butt of a Glock peeked out from beneath her leather jacket. Apparently network security was more dangerous than sitting in front of a computer screen. Or had Elizabeth been assigned guard duty?

The former NSA consultant tapped her black-painted fingernails against the chair railing. "He's the most guarded man I've ever met, but if there's one thing I know about Anthony Harris, it's that a knife wound to the ribs and a bullet to the leg won't stop him from doing his job."

Glennon's spine tingled. She'd gotten that right. That'd been one of the two reasons she'd called him for help in the first place. The man had been sculpted from steel and infused with a determination like no other. Like the good Ranger he was supposed to be. As for the other reason… Heat crawled up her neck. She ran her hand through her hair as a distraction.

"But I should tell you, he's not going to be very happy when he wakes up," Elizabeth said.

"What do you mean?" Glennon straightened in the bed. Had he changed his mind? Would she have to find Bennett on her own now that they'd discovered Mascaro's involvement in her partner's disappearance? She swallowed hard. If the past two days revealed anything about this investigation, it was that she couldn't do this on her own.

"During the firefight downtown, something happened." Elizabeth reached into her jacket pocket, her expression guarded. She extracted a tangle of titanium. Shoving to her feet, she crossed the room and offered the mess to Glennon. Short dark hair hid her expression. "And I'm not sure what he'll do when he finds out about it."

Recognition flared. Anthony's favorite pair of aviator sunglasses. The exact pair she'd gifted him once upon a time had been destroyed. Lenses cracked, one earpiece missing completely. A laugh bubbled up

Glennon's throat. "I can't believe he still has these."
Well, had. She ran the pad of her thumb over the
tinted glass. "I bought them for him right after I
graduated basic training."

He'd kept them after all this time. Just as he'd
kept her engagement ring around his neck. Her head
pounded. Damn it. This was supposed to be easy.
She'd had a plan. Find Bennett. Resign from the
Military Police. Put in her discharge papers and get
on with her life. Her and Hunter. The two of them
against the world. That was it.

But now... Anthony was there. Protecting her.
Risking his life for her. Resurrecting a part of her
she hadn't expected to feel ever again.

And now he'd been centered in crosshairs meant
for her.

Because of her.

"What about the shooter?" she asked.

The lighting from behind the bed sharpened the
edges of the Elizabeth's jawline. "What shooter?"

Her throat tightened. Glennon struggled to swallow and she could only imagine how bad the bruises
on her neck looked. "We were ambushed. He ran us
off the road."

"The team has been scouring that scene for the
past eight hours with Anchorage PD," Elizabeth said.
"There wasn't any evidence of a shooter."

Air rushed from her lungs. He'd gotten away?

"Then I need to get out of here." Glennon set the

sunglasses on the bedside table and threw back the sheets. She pulled the catheters and monitors from her skin. Rushing to collect her clothes from the nook under the window, she spun toward the bathroom. "I've wasted enough time when I should be out there looking for my partner."

"I can see why Anthony's broken Sullivan's number one rule for you." Elizabeth's voice stopped her cold. "You're as stubborn as he is."

Glennon turned. "What rule?"

"We're warned about falling for our clients or co-workers." Elizabeth stood, crossing her arms across her middle. The gun inhibited some of her movement, but the network analyst didn't seem to mind. Might've even been used to it. "Causes too many problems with our assignments. Once emotions get involved, makes it hard for us to focus on the job. Leads to risks that might've been avoided in the first place."

Elizabeth wanted to talk about risks? The tiny muscles along Glennon's jaw jerked. She'd risked everything—her job, her partner, her life—in going to Anthony for help. If she hadn't? The price would've been far greater. Not just for her but for everyone in her life.

"Sounds like you've learned from personal experience." Besides, Anthony wasn't falling for her. Couldn't be. Not after what she'd done to him. Not after dragging him into this mess, after putting his life in danger. Glennon shook her head, thankful the rapid flutter of her heart rate couldn't register on the screens anymore. None of this had been part of the plan. A blast of cold air from the vent above reminded her how exposed she was standing there in only a thin sheet of a gown. How vulnerable. She hugged her still damp clothing—and her empty shoulder holster—tighter. "I thought you were the computer expert. Not the profiler."

"I don't need to get inside Anthony's head to see something clearly staring me in the face." Elizabeth headed for the door. Wrenching the thick door open, she turned back, frozen in the doorway. "Be careful, Glennon. If anybody on this team is compromised, we're all at risk. And so are our clients."

Elizabeth disappeared into the hallway.

She was right. Glennon clutched her clothing tighter. Letting old feelings come between her and Anthony, letting him in again, would endanger them both. The investigation. That was all that mattered. All that *could* matter.

She pushed her legs into her jeans and finished dressing as fast as she could. Her army credentials had been set on the table beside the bed. Hospital administration had most likely registered her into the system using her ID. The army would know she'd been here, had probably already sent someone for her. The marshal wasn't the only compromised operative in Nicholas Mascaro's unit. The two shooters from the garage had been military. So she didn't have much time.

Where was her service weapon?

Palming her credentials into her hand, Glennon paused as she reached for Anthony's broken sunglasses. Every second she wasted in this room stacked against her chances of recovering Bennett, but she didn't move. Couldn't. Anthony had broken Blackhawk Security's number one rule. For her.

Her forehead throbbed as she backed toward the door, leaving the sunglasses behind. If she left now—

The door swung inward. "Going somewhere?"

Anxiety flooded the muscles down her spine. That voice... She closed her eyes, committing it to memory all over again. Glennon tamped down the need to hear his heart beat against her ear, to confirm for herself he was okay. "Elizabeth told you I was leaving."

"You hired me to protect you." He stood directly behind her. How had he moved so quietly? So quickly? Anthony's voice dipped into dangerous territory. "I don't stop when I'm tired or injured. I only stop when the job is done. And I'm not done with you."

A tremor chased across her back, loosening the small muscles down her spine. She automatically leaned toward him, her weight shifting onto her heels. That pull he had on her... She'd always been weak when he'd gotten so close. Tendrils of his controlled exhalations raised the hairs on the back of her neck. All she had to do was fall. And he'd catch her. He'd already proved as much over the last few days. So why did the thought of taking that final leap paralyze her to the core?

Elizabeth's claims echoed through her mind. Emotional attachment brought risk, could compromise the entire team. And no matter how much she wanted—no, *needed*—that human connection right now, Glennon couldn't risk the fall. He'd left her without a net once. She wouldn't let it happen again. "Is that all you see me as? A job?"

That would make moving on after the investigation a lot easier.

"I want you, Glennon. Always have." The words were nearly a growl from between his lips. He moved into her, his chest pressed against her spine. Predatory. Dangerous. But at his core, Anthony was a man who'd fight desperately for his clients. Fight for her. His body heat tunneled beneath her clothing, chasing away the myriad aches and pains. "We're in this together. Until the end. And I'll be damned if I let you walk out of my life again."

Chapter Nine

Hypothermia. Stab wound. Bullet wound in his thigh. It would've been a hell of a way to die.

But all of that vanished with Glennon turning into him, her rosy scent spreading through his system. He'd meant every word. Every cell in his body, every thought, wanted her. Always had. What that meant for their future—if they even had a future—he didn't know. But he wasn't about to lose her all over again. Not without a fight.

The bruise on her forehead had faded slightly, but guilt ate at him. He framed her jawline, running the pad of his thumb across the lump where her head had hit the steering wheel. To her credit, she didn't flinch. First the bullet in her shoulder then the head wound. Some kind of bodyguard she'd hired. "I'm sorry I didn't take better care of you."

"I'm alive, aren't I? That's what I hired you to do." Brilliant green eyes locked on him. A small curl of one side of her mouth brought his attention to her lips. How in the world could she stand there as though they hadn't just been through hell and back? "But in the future, not dying while we're trying to escape a pair of corrupt soldiers would help your cause."

A laugh rumbled through his chest. Right. She'd saved his life, too, hadn't she? Dragging his ass out of that garage while dodging an onslaught of bullets couldn't have been easy. Her determination to get the job done had saved his life. No matter the risk. "Guess that makes us even."

"Not even close, Ranger. You…" She dropped her hand, her smile disappearing, but didn't move away. Her shoulders rose on a strong inhale, color draining from her features. "I thought you were going to die. All that blood—"

"I owe you my life." He closed the slight distance between them.

She lifted her gaze to his. Her expression said she didn't believe him.

Anthony set his hands on her hips, locking her against him. He understood. All too easily, those agonizing seconds of panic, the memories of almost losing her as he'd fought to expel the water from her lungs rushed to the front of his mind. And he never wanted to think about them again.

He moved slowly, giving her a chance to escape. Planting his mouth below her earlobe, he inhaled as much of her as he could, making her a part of him.

Forever. "We survived. Together. That's all that matters."

Glennon nodded into his chest but hesitation stiffened the muscles along her back. "I just... Not knowing if you were going to make it out of that garage alive, if I could get you the help you needed, were the worst seconds of my life. I never want to go through that again."

"Keep talking like that and I'll think you care about me, sweetheart." The steady thump of his heart pulsed into his left ribs and thigh. Nearly sixty stitches ached as they stood there in the middle of her hospital room, but Anthony didn't dare move. He'd stay in this moment forever if she'd let him, hold on to her as long as he could. Pretend nothing bad waited outside those hospital doors. Pain be damned. She was worth every agonizing second. He slid his fingers beneath her jaw, notching her chin higher. "I'm not going anywhere."

"Good. Because I can't do this by myself. I don't want to do this by myself." She passed her tongue across the small cut in her lower lip. "I need you."

"You have me. You always have." The control he'd held on to so tightly since that first kiss in her barracks drained from his veins. Anthony crushed her against his chest, his mouth on hers, his fingertips digging into her lower back. Careful of each and every wound, he memorized the one woman who could break him inch by slow, agonizing inch. The remnants of spearmint exploded across his tongue as he explored her mouth. Fresh. Invigorating.

Damn, he'd missed this. Missed her. Desire barreled through him, tightening the muscles down his back and across his shoulders. He kissed her slowly, carefully, savoring every move of her mouth against his as he threaded his fingers through the base of her ponytail. Forget her missing partner. Forget Nicholas Mascaro. Forget the past. All he needed was Glennon. Here. Now. Forever. His lungs worked overtime to keep up with his racing heartbeat. He'd let her slip away once, but the truth rang clear as he broke the kiss. He'd kill to keep her by his side.

Hell, he already had. And he'd pull that trigger all over again if it meant she stayed here.

"This is a bad idea." Stiffening, she pulled away, running one hand through her hair. She did that a lot. Used that single action to distance herself from him. Emotionally. Physically. But she wouldn't get away that easily. Not this time. "It's not part of the plan."

"And at exactly what point in your plan did you expect to be shot, get run off the road by a contracted soldier, and drown in Turnagain Arm?" he asked.

"You make a valid point." A laugh burst from between her lips and she pressed her fingertips to the cut at one corner. "Do you remember anything after the crash? I hit my head pretty hard. It's still all a bit fuzzy."

Anthony let her take a step back. His skin cooled

at the loss of her natural heat, but he'd remember the feel of her pressed against him. Forever. "Bits and pieces."

The memories of those final moments before his body had finally shut down had replayed in his head over and over since he'd woken in his room a few hours ago. How could he possibly tell her the truth? This entire investigation—her investigation—depended on her partner's innocence. On Sergeant Bennett Spencer being Mascaro's target, as Glennon had become.

Only they'd been wrong from the start.

"Elizabeth said the police couldn't find any evidence of the shooter that followed us out of the garage. How is that possible?" she asked. "Some Good Samaritan witnessed the whole thing but he never saw the shooter and his accomplice in the Mack truck run us off the road in the first place?"

Good Samaritan? That wasn't how Anthony remembered it. He curled his fingers into his palm. Damn it. He couldn't hide this from her. If they were going to find Bennett and put an end to this investigation, he had to tell her the truth. "There is no Good Samaritan. The driver of the truck isn't working with the shooter. He *killed* the shooter."

Glennon froze for a split second, one hand fastened around the back of her neck. "How do you know that?"

"After I resuscitated you on the shoreline, the shooter came to finish the job." Pressure built behind his sternum. He'd fought like hell to get to his weapon, but he'd been helpless. Worthless. Now that he thought about it, Anthony supposed he owed the driver a thank-you. "He didn't get the chance."

"Why would the driver do that?" She sank onto the edge of the hospital bed, her gaze distant, questioning. "If they weren't working together, why run us off the road in the first place? Why drive us to the hospital? It doesn't make sense."

No. It didn't. But in a missing persons investigation, there were no easy answers. And she wasn't about to like his next one, either. "Bennett Spencer was driving the Mack truck, Glennon. *He* ran us off the highway. He killed the shooter before the bastard had a chance to abduct you."

Her attention snapped to him, lips parting on a strong exhale, features smooth. Her white-knuckled grip tightened on the edge of the mattress. "That son of a bitch. I knew it."

She knew what, exactly? "I just told you I recognized your partner as the man driving the truck who ran us off the road, and that he killed one of Mascaro's operatives. And that makes sense to you?"

"I was going to wait until I was sure…" She pushed to her feet, one hand diving into her jacket pocket then out again. Her fingers uncurled and centered in her palm was a small American flag pin. It wasn't anything special, available at any drugstore, but it obviously held some kind of significance. She wouldn't have kept it otherwise. "I found this at your cabin. After the operative broke in."

"Is this supposed to mean something to me?" Anthony took the pin, his fingertips sliding against her palm. A surge of awareness shot up his arm, resurrecting only a sliver of the desire burning through his veins, but Glennon didn't seem to notice. Or was she focused on the pin to avoid looking at him?

"No, but it means something to me. It's Bennett's." She nodded toward the evidence—evidence she'd kept secret from him for two days. "He's kept it in his desk drawer as long as I can remember. It was his sister's. Never wore it, never told me why he'd held on to it after all these years, but it was important to him." Glennon crossed her arms over her chest. Shaking her head, she turned away from him as a hint of pink colored her face and neck. "I couldn't find it after he went missing. Now I know why."

"Because the marshal was telling the truth." Anthony's stomach dropped. Hell. Things were about to get bloodier and messier. With Glennon centered in the middle of it all. "Bennett is part of Mascaro's crew."

"Looks that way. So you have a choice. You can return to your surveillance assignments and get back the life you had before I added you to Mascaro's hit list. Or you can help me bring the bastards down. All of them. Bennett included." Red tinged her cheeks.

"Either way, I have to go. What's it going to be, Ranger?"

"When have you ever known me to shy away from a fight?" He handed the pin back to her and patted himself for weapons. The staff had confiscated everything when Sergeant Spencer had dumped them at the hospital's front door. They were going to have to make a pit stop. "Just tell me where we're going."

"At the moment, to get my gun back." Glennon rushed past him, her shoulder clipping his arm. She ripped open the door. Half turning her face toward him, she froze. "Then to protect my son."

How could Bennett do this to her? Two years as partners. She'd trusted him with her life, trusted him with her secret. She'd let him inside her house, made him part of her son's life. Uncle Bennett. What was she supposed to tell Hunter now? Pressure built in her chest as she ground her back teeth together. Bennett had known everything about her. Obviously she couldn't say the same for him. She was an investigator, for crying out loud. How could she not have seen the truth?

Glennon kept her footsteps light as she approached the house, weapon in hand. Fanning her fingers over the gun's grip, she exhaled hard. Her pulse beat loudly in her ears. Mascaro had already sent hit men after her and Anthony. But she'd kill every last one of them before they laid a finger on her son.

"You're blaming yourself." The mountain of muscle close on her heels had her back, even with the slight limp he fought to hide from her.

"Did the Rangers train you to read minds or is that a new skill of yours?" Anthony had had a choice back at the hospital and he'd chosen to follow her into battle. She should've been relieved. She had a better chance of bringing down the crew responsible for putting that bullet in his leg with him at her side, but… The butterflies in her stomach spread through her entire system. She hadn't prepared for this day. Imagined it? Sure. But those had only been fantasies. This…this was real. She swallowed hard, took a deep breath. Anthony was about to meet her son. Holstering her weapon, Glennon knocked on the faded red door, her muscles strung tight.

"I don't need to be able to read minds to know what's going through your head. I know exactly what you're thinking, sweetheart." His deep, rumbling laugh vibrated through her, he was so close. The scent of soap and man clouded her senses over the freezing air around them, but she couldn't help but breathe a bit deeper. Wisps of his breath tickled the back of her neck. "There was no way you could've known about your partner. Bennett is a double agent. And he's obviously very good at his job."

From inside, footsteps echoed off the house's original hardwood floors.

A gust of blistering cold brushed against her

as she turned into him. He didn't understand. She wasn't blaming herself. "I'm not ashamed I didn't see him for what he really was. I'm pissed off."

The door swung open, the racking of a shotgun shell loud in her ears.

Glennon froze but didn't raise her weapon. Physical tension radiated off Anthony as he moved to her side. Holstering her Glock, she smiled at the woman on the other end of the gun. "Hi, Mom."

Green eyes, nearly the exact same color as hers, narrowed on her then widened. The older woman lowered the shotgun an inch but kept her wrinkled grip tight around the weapon. While other moms were teaching their daughters how to braid their hair or how to put together the perfect outfit for the first day of school, Helen Chase had been teaching her daughter how to assemble and disassemble that same shotgun on the kitchen table. Blindfolded. Of the few good memories Glennon had of her childhood, those were her favorite. Just her and her mom. The two of them against the world. "You forget something? You're not supposed to show up here unannounced, girl. That was part of our deal."

Helen's thick East Kentucky accent warmed Glennon through and through. Damn, it felt good to be home. She dropped her hands to her sides as another gust of cold uprooted a corner of her mother's signature flannel long-sleeved shirt. "I came to make sure my son is safe. You can put the gun down now."

"I told you I'd protect him with my life and I meant it," Helen said.

Another deep laugh vibrated through Anthony's chest. He nodded at the older woman, a mixture of respect and amusement etched into his expression. "Helen. Been a while."

The shotgun found a new target as her mother swung it toward him. Helen's gaze never left his as she cocked her head. "*This* is who you hired to help you bring down those bastards who came after you and my grandson? Girl, I thought I taught you more sense than that. Didn't what happened between me and your daddy teach you anything?"

"Excuse me?" Anthony's voice dipped into dangerous territory. The weight of his gaze pressed the air from Glennon's lungs as he spun on her. "I'm going to forget the part where Helen compared me to your deadbeat asshole father. Mascaro's men came after you and Hunter *before* you hired me?"

Damn it. Glennon stiffened.

"Wasn't important at the time." The sound of broken glass hitting tile, her reaching for the combat knife she kept under her pillow and extracting her service weapon from the gun safe under her bed slid through her mind. She and Hunter had made it out of the house just fine. They'd holed up in a hotel room the rest of the night after she'd called the police. She'd then informed the marshal she and Bennett would be looking into a missing shipment of weapons at JBER and left for Anchorage the second her

CO had approved. "I didn't know who broke into my house or if it had anything to do with our investigation. I still don't."

"How about you let me decide what's important to this investigation from now on?" Anthony gripped his beard, pulling at the hair. He had a point. First, Bennett's American flag pin. Now this. He had every right not to trust her right now. "Anything else you're not telling me?"

She flushed as Helen's attention drifted from Anthony straight to her. She silently screamed for her mother to keep her mouth shut. Now wasn't the time. Not here. Not yet.

"Well, hell. Looks like you two still have a few things to work out. But it's best not to make yourselves easy targets standing out here in the cold." Helen lowered the shotgun barrel toward the floor and cleared the doorway. "Come on then. Get inside."

A wall of hot air slammed against Glennon as they walked through the door. The cold had never bothered her, but the blistering ice in Anthony's eyes froze her to the core. Her throat tightened. This day kept getting better and better.

A familiar combination of her mother's perfume and the lingering scent of home-fried chicken sank deep into her lungs. She hadn't set foot in this house in years, but the living room, dining room, kitchen— all had remained the same. No family photos hung on the walls, destroyed years ago in a fire. Barely any personal effects adorned the space. The only thing that had changed? The shelf of countless liquor bottles her father had kept stocked was empty. Glennon glanced at her mother.

No. Helen shouldn't have compared Anthony to her father. Their situations weren't the same. The man at her side would never drink himself into a rage and take it out on his family. In fact, given the chance, she'd bet the former Ranger would have more than a few words for the man who'd left his wife's and daughter's lives in ruins. She'd always known a part of her—some small, distant part—had urged her to join the Military Police so she could track the deadbeat down for what he'd done. But the past was better left buried. She studied the Ranger at her side, then spun on the edge of the worn area rug.

"Can't remember the last time you were in this house." Her mother's fierce green eyes landed on her and an understanding passed between them.

Glennon nodded. They both knew why she hadn't come home. Too many bad memories. "Where's Hunter?"

"Asleep in your old room. He likes it in there. Hardly ever leaves." Her mother set the gun upright against the wall beside the front door. Wasn't the only one, either. Over the years, Helen Chase had collected an entire arsenal to protect her home and her family. She secured the front door and armed the alarm. Although she hadn't smoked in years, deep lines creased the edges of Helen's mouth. "He's been asking about you, wants to know when you're coming to take him home."

Home. Hell, Glennon didn't even know where that was anymore. Back in Stafford, Virginia? Here, in Anchorage? Anthony turned as he surveyed the rest of the house in her peripheral vision, her awareness of him at an all-time high. She'd promised to keep her emotions in check before hiring him to protect her—for her son's sake—but after what had happened back in the garage, almost losing him... Her stomach sank. Truth was, he was more than a bodyguard. Always had been.

"This thing that we're doing... These people." Bennett's features flashed across her mind. "It's more complicated than I thought."

"So you said over the phone two nights ago." Helen fisted her hands on her hips, her weight shifting onto one side. "I told you I'd protect Hunter with everything I got so you can do what you gotta do, but I need to know. What exactly have you gotten yourself into, girl?"

"I can't tell you. Not yet, anyway." She swallowed the urge to reveal everything. The dead sniper, Bennett's involvement in Nicholas Mascaro's operation, how very close she was to losing her tightly held control. She glanced at Anthony and rolled her fingers into her palms. A couple more days. That was all she needed to end this nightmare. "But I promise, it's almost over. I just wanted to make sure he was okay."

Anthony lowered his chin to his chest, glancing back at her over his shoulder. "Hallway."

"Grandma—" small footsteps scuffed against the hardwood floor down the hall "—I need water and ice in my cup, please."

Warmth shot through Glennon as a head of short blond hair came into sight. A familiar pair of worn Batman pajamas and bright green eyes cleared the adrenalized haze of the last few days. Air rushed from her lungs. Her eyes burned. "Hey, baby."

Hunter's attention snapped to her, his eyes widening, mouth dropping open. "Mommy!"

The living room blurred in her vision as she closed the distance between them. Landing hard on her knees, Glennon wrapped Hunter in her arms. The pain in her shoulder pulled at her but she pushed it to the back of her mind. "I missed you."

"I missed you, too." His thin, four-year-old arms tightened around her neck.

An invisible weight of relief bore into her. She lifted her gaze to Anthony, surprised to find the rough edges that had sharpened his features for so long had softened. Pulling back slightly, she framed Hunter's small face between her hands. The butterflies in her gut rebelled in full force. She exhaled to expel the burning sensation exploding in her chest. This was it. This was her chance to tell the truth. "Hunter, baby, I have a friend here I want you to meet."

Chapter Ten

He'd never stood a chance.

Years of intense training, combat operations, losing trusted friends and facing off with death more times than he could count hadn't done him a damn bit of good. Glennon Chase had always been the one war he couldn't fight.

And he didn't want to. Not anymore.

A smile brightened the darkness that had been permanently etched on her features since he'd set sights on her. Chasing her son around the coffee table, Glennon roared at the top of her lungs. For the past hour, she and Hunter had taken turns succumbing to the tickle monster. Their combined laughter had even reached him outside while he'd conducted a perimeter check, and he couldn't keep from smiling. They were perfect together—a family—but an imagined vice tightened his chest nonetheless.

"They make quite the pair, don't they?" Helen handed him a fresh cup of coffee then pushed her shoulder into the wall beside him. She shifted her weight from one leg to the other. Must be one of her old injuries from her married days acting up. "I was surprised to find you standing next to her out there on my porch. So how'd she do it? How'd she convince you to help her after what she did?"

He straightened, the coffee swishing against the side of his mug. "Hunter."

"She tell you who his daddy is?" she asked.

"No." Did it matter?

Helen nodded in his peripheral vision. "You know, I'd never met my grandson until a couple of weeks ago." She took a sip of her coffee, her swallow audible. "Glennon wouldn't come back here after growing up the way she did. Couldn't even step foot in this house until tonight. Can't say I blame her." Helen shifted again, her long, grayish-blond hair swinging forward. "But you didn't come back here to listen to me ramble on about the past. It's the future that matters, don't it?"

Damn straight. And his entire future had just started running around the couches for another game of tickle monster. Heat worked into his hand as he stared into the watery black reflection of the coffee. He forced the small muscles around his eyes to relax and sipped from his mug, the dark, rich liquid burning his throat on the way down. The taste escaped him as Glennon and her son collapsed into a pile of giggles on the living room floor. He'd already experienced as much evil in the world as he could tolerate. This right here? This perfect little family? That was what he'd wanted since the moment he'd set eyes on her back in his teaching days. It was everything. She was everything.

"She's strong. Stronger than I was at her age." Helen's lips thinned into a hard line, the wrinkles around her mouth growing deeper. "She's a big-time investigator now, but whatever this is she's wrapped up in—" she nodded toward Glennon "—I need you to get her out of it, Anthony. I need you to do what you've got to do to make sure my daughter comes home to that boy, understand?"

No question. While he'd initially fought against getting wrapped up in the one woman he never thought he'd see again, he'd made his decision the second he'd recognized her voice over the phone. He'd never given up on her. Never intended to let her go, but he'd kept his distance. Hadn't looked for her. Out of respect.

The weight of her engagement ring against his skin pulled at his attention. No. He wasn't about to lose her again. And as for Mascaro's crew? They could have her over his dead body. Glennon was his. Forever. "You have my word."

"Anthony, save me!" Hunter's call was drowned in a flood of laughter as his mother clamped her hand over his mouth from behind.

Hesitation gripped him hard. His drumming

heartbeat was too loud behind his ears. Haiti, Bosnia, Kosovo. None of those operations had trained him for this. What was he supposed to do? The little boy he'd met not an hour ago wanted him to join in his game.

"Go on now." Helen took the cup from his hand. "He's promised me he's not biting people anymore. But I'd keep your fingers out of his mouth just in case."

What was one more scar?

"Understood." All right then. This was it. Anthony nodded as he stripped out of his shoulder holster and set it on top of a bookcase to his right. Next, the blades he kept strapped at his ankle and thigh. After unloading his entire arsenal, he was ready. Advancing onto the battlefield, he dove straight into action. His entire body heated as Glennon smiled up at him from her position on the floor. Screw the stitches. Seeing these two so happy when everything in his life centered around guns, blood and betrayal was all that mattered. His control crumbled as another round of laughs exploded around him. "I never leave a man behind."

Hunter fought against his mother's hold, his small, crooked smile wide. "Get her!"

"And get on your mom's bad side? I don't think so." Anthony went in for the attack, aiming straight for Hunter's underarms.

A high-pitched scream nearly burst his eardrums

as the four-year-old lifted his feet to kick out. Anthony dodged the first attempt but caught a hit to the gut the second time around. Hunter fell onto his back, sandwiching Glennon between her son and the floor. Right where he wanted her. Crooking his finger, Anthony whispered the plan in Hunter's ear. "Got it?"

Hunter nodded, spinning into his mother. In two seconds flat the boy pinned her wrists against the floor. Faux screams filled the living room as Glennon fought against her son's strength. "Got you!"

"Wait! You weren't supposed to go until three." Anthony shrugged. "Tickle her!"

The four-year-old didn't have to be told twice, consumed with the need to make his mother laugh.

Tucking her chin against her chest, Glennon curled into a fetal position, but that wouldn't save her. Not from him.

Anthony maneuvered around the other side of the fight. Wrapping his grip around one wrist, he hauled her off the floor and against him, her back to his chest. Her rosy scent filled the living room as he lifted her uninjured arm above her head. She was exposed. Vulnerable. "Now, Hunter! Go, go, go!"

"No!" Her spine tensed as her son took advantage. She fought to pull her arm down, to get away from him, her laugh smooth and addictive in every sense of the word. "This isn't fair. There are two of you and only one of me."

He committed the sound to memory. Lowering his mouth to her ear, Anthony inhaled her scent deep into his system. No matter what happened at the end of the investigation, he would have this. If only for a night, he'd made her smile, made her laugh. She'd been happy. "Haven't you heard, all is fair in love and war?"

"Oh, it is on." She kicked at the floor and launched them backward. The maneuver broke his hold on her wrists and she spun into him. Wrapping her arms around his middle, Glennon rolled them across the worn rug with a lightness he'd never seen in her before. The living room blurred in his vision then vanished altogether, his entire focus centered on her. The danger that awaited them outside that front door, the betrayal of the past three days, had vanished the second she'd laid eyes on her son.

The ache in his chest lessened as he pinned her beneath his weight, her expression bright and full of something he hadn't seen in a long time. Hope. Her chest rose and fell against his as she fought to catch her breath. A fleeting smile burst across her features as she brushed away a stray piece of hair that had caught in her long lashes. "You two might've won this round, but this isn't over. We're not finished."

"You got that right, sweetheart." Seconds slipped by as he stared down at her, but the sudden onslaught of forty pounds of deadweight crushing him into Glennon cleared his head. Reaching back, he rolled away from her as he maneuvered the laughing four-year-old into his arms. He fell back against the nearest couch, fought to catch his breath. Pain surged through the wound in his side. "Oh, man. You got me."

"All right, boy." Helen rounded the corner from the kitchen, securing the lid on Hunter's cup into place. She hiked one hand onto her hip and offered him the drink. "I filled up your water. Time to get your tiny butt back in bed."

Hunter's drawn-out groan pulled a laugh from Anthony's chest.

"Listen to Grandma, baby." Glennon shoved to her feet. "It's way past your bedtime."

"Okay." Eyes downcast, feet dragging across the rug, Hunter closed the distance between him and his mother, giving her a tight hug good-night. "When will we be going home?"

Anthony's stomach sank.

Glennon raised her gaze to his from over her son's shoulder. The light speckling of freckles across her nose darkened as color drained from her face. "Soon, baby. Mommy just has one more thing she needs to do."

"Okay. Be careful. Don't get hurt again." Hunter released his hold, turning toward Anthony with one hand raised. "Bye."

"Bye, buddy." Anthony offered a high-five as he

caught Glennon wipe her hand across her cheek. "I had fun playing with you. We'll do it again, okay?"

With an overexaggerated nod and a quick pit stop to grab his drink from Helen, the four-year-old Caped Crusader disappeared down the hallway with his grandmother close behind.

"That's the second time I've had to leave him here. He doesn't understand why." Glennon sank onto the floor, devastation etched into her expression as she stared after her son. Sniffling, she shook her head. "Not sure you're cut out for playing with my son again." She nodded at his wound. "You're bleeding."

Anthony pulled his shirt away from his skin, the spreading red stain across his T-shirt registering. Damn it. He must've torn a few stitches wrestling across the floor. A rough laugh shook through him. "He's definitely stronger than he looks."

"That, he is. Come on. My mom has a sewing kit around here somewhere." Glennon offered him her hand. "We'll get you stitched back up then go over our next move to find Bennett."

"There won't be much to go over. I've already worked it out." Sliding his hand into hers, Anthony ignored the sting in his side and stood. "Your partner started this war. We're going to end it."

A SKY FULL of pinks, greens and oranges—and Anthony was staring at her.

Puffs of air crystallized in front of her mouth as they took position in the tree line surrounding the cabin. A chill swept up her spine, but not from the dropping temperature. Not even from the anticipation of their target walking into Anthony's crosshairs. Because, after all these years, her heart still skipped a beat at the sight of him.

She swallowed hard, lying on the tarp and blanket they'd brought to protect them from the snow. Aurora borealis danced above them, providing a minuscule amount of light, but Anthony had trained for operations exactly like this as a Ranger. He didn't need daylight to locate his target. He'd get the job done, even with a brand-new set of stitches in his side. "It's going to be hard to spot our target if you keep staring at me."

"I'm good at multitasking." One edge of his mouth turned upward. He'd armed himself with his favored Beretta, set up a sniper rifle and strapped on a combat knife, but the most fearsome weapon he held was that minefield of a smile. He pressed his left eye against the scope, relieving a bit of the pressure that had built in her chest.

"If you say so. Just remember you've already used up the saving-your-life coupon from me, so I'd focus if I were you." Glennon forced herself to study the span of property between them and the cabin. To prove she could. The trap was set. All she'd had to do was turn on her army-issued phone after coming back to the cabin and wait. With Campbell Lake to their right and a wide expanse of nothing but snow in front of them, they had the best view of anyone coming to collect on Staff Sergeant Mascaro's contract on her head. Whoever that might be.

Danger edged closer; she could feel it. Cold worked through her thick coat, down into her bones. She scanned the woods surrounding them for movement.

"Hell, I've missed you." The words were rough, rumbly and so low she hadn't been entirely sure she'd heard him right.

She jerked her gaze back to his face. "What?"

Anthony shifted his trigger finger alongside the rifle. "You know me better than anyone, Glennon, even my team. And I don't believe in giving up." He kept his eye pressed to the scope. "Especially not when it comes to us."

She didn't know what to say to that. He wanted to have this discussion now? In the middle of the wilderness as they waited for Mascaro's men? She surveyed the landscape for signs of another soldier coming to collect the price on her head. "And you think now is the time to have this conversation?"

"When else are we going to find a time we're not being shot at or hunted down?"

Okay. He had a point.

Dark blue eyes centered on her, compressing the frigid air locked in her lungs. "You're the best investigator I've ever met. You're insanely smart, you'll do anything for the people who matter most to you and you're not afraid to stand up for what's right."

Her insides warmed, counteracting the numbness taking root in her fingers and toes.

"Why are you telling me this?" She licked her dry lips, a minor mistake out here in below-freezing temperatures, but she couldn't think. Couldn't breathe. Anxiety clawed an ugly path up her throat. "What do you want from me?"

"Everything, sweetheart." The tendons along the line of his neck flexed. "When this investigation is over, I want you and Hunter to stay here, in Anchorage, with me. I don't care what you're hiding. I can handle every single secret you have."

Her heart iced, her lips tingling with numbness. No. He couldn't. Because the second she revealed the truth, he'd walk away. He'd hate her. Nausea rolled in her stomach. And then who would she have? Everyone else in her life had already betrayed her. Her heartbeat drummed too loud in her ears as she pushed to her feet. She curled her fingers into the palms of her thick gloves in an attempt to bring some blood flow back. She couldn't risk losing him. Not Anthony. Not yet.

Space. She needed to put space between them. "I have to go."

"Glennon, wait." His brows drew inward a split second before she cleared the tree line.

The sound of crunching snow followed close on her heels as she waded through the brush. A strong grip wrapped around her biceps. The world blurred as he spun her around. Anthony pressed her into his chest, held her up as her knees shook. He'd left the rifle in position behind him, abandoning his post. "You left me once. I'll be damned if I let it happen again without good reason."

He still had his fingers wrapped around her arm, and her breath hitched. Even through her winter gear, he could make her feel too much. Her body's response to Anthony had always been off the charts. She was too attuned to him. Too sensitive. And that was a very dangerous thing.

"I left because you weren't there when I needed you the most." The gut-wrenching shift in his expression filled her with dread. His hold lightened. She swallowed hard, the words much sharper than she'd intended, but she had to make one thing clear. This wasn't just about the two of them. "And if it happened again, it wouldn't only affect me. Do you understand?"

The dimple almost completely hidden beneath his beard deepened. "I would never do *anything* to hurt Hunter."

"I believe you. Now. And I think you believe that, too." A blast of Arctic chill swept through her, hammering at her already exhausted defenses. Physically. Emotionally. "But what's to stop you from re-upping for another tour or deciding your assignments with Blackhawk Security are more important than us?"

The blue in his eyes dimmed. He seemed so

much…bigger in that moment. Dangerous, even. But Anthony would never hurt her. Hell, he'd taken a bullet for her. Luck had nothing to do with her standing there. She'd cheated death. Because of the Grim Reaper. But still, he didn't answer.

Glennon nodded. "I barely kept my head above water when I left Anchorage, Anthony. I won't put my son through that. And if this means you can't help me anymore, I won't hold it against you."

Her boots sank into soft powder as she turned away, slowing her escape. But she wouldn't stop. Couldn't. No matter how much she wanted to go back, to slip into his hold, they didn't have a future together. Soon, the investigation into Mascaro would be over and she'd go back to CID headquarters in Quantico. Where she belonged.

The weight of his gaze drilled into her from behind as she climbed the cabin's front steps. He hadn't followed her. She should've been relieved, but the tingling in her arm—where he'd touched her—spread fast.

Shouldering her way inside, Glennon exhaled the remnants of his clean, masculine scent from her system. She pressed her spine into the thick wooden door. Sweat built underneath her clothing, but it had nothing to do with the flames simmering in the fireplace a few feet away. She'd done the right thing. Pain shot through the back of her skull as her head hit the door. She closed her eyes. "I did the right thing."

Swiping a glove under her nose, she tossed her

winter gear over the back of the couch and escaped
to the guest bedroom. Having another door between
them wouldn't erase the past ten minutes from her
memory, but it would help to relieve the urge to
march back out there in below-freezing conditions.
That wouldn't do any good. What more was there
to discuss?

Stay with me.

Why did that idea feel so…right? Whatever she
felt for him now wasn't real. At least, not anymore.
She'd fallen in love with him years ago. Her feelings—however clouded—were an echo of that time.
Had nothing to do with the last three days. Had nothing to do with the fact he'd stood by her side, protected her, saved her life. Had nothing to do with
the way he'd gotten Hunter to laugh or given her
son a pass on tearing open his stitches. Floorboards
groaned under her weight as she paced to the cur-
tained window. Did it?

A laugh burst up her throat. She was Military Police, for crying out loud. Yet here she was, hiding.
Hiding from the truth. Glennon ran a hand through
her hair, turning at the sound of heavy boot steps
coming down the hallway. Soft beeping reached her
ears. Anthony had set the alarm. A door closed softly,
followed by the sound of running water. The shower.
She was kidding herself. Of course she'd started falling back in love with him. How could she not?

Anthony Harris was the kind of man any soldier
would be lucky to have by her side, the kind of man

who loved fiercely and protected loyally. She exhaled hard. Hell, she couldn't believe she was doing this. Glennon ripped open the bedroom door. He was the kind of man who could make her forget the nightmare around her, if only for a night.

Steam worked its way from underneath the bathroom door. The bright red light on Anthony's new security alarm panel said the cabin was secure. Mascaro's crew wouldn't get in without her knowing, but hesitation still gripped her hard, her hand positioned over the doorknob. One twist. That was all it would take. She could have everything she'd ever wanted. The chance to have a real family. One breath. Two. Shouldering her way inside, Glennon froze.

Standing outside the shower, stripped down to nothing but a pair of dark cargo pants, Anthony stood as though he'd expected her. Ridges and valleys shifted across his bare abdomen as he tossed his shirt to the tile floor. The tattoo she'd traced countless times twisted up his arm. Death Before Dishonor. And wasn't that the perfect representation of a Ranger. "Glennon, I—"

"I don't want to talk." A slow exhale escaped her control as she met his gaze. Unflinching. Bare. Vulnerable. Taking a single step forward, she gripped the edge of her T-shirt, lifting it over her head. Her hair fell in loose strands around her face. Discarding her shirt, she removed her boots using her heels. "Tonight, I only want you."

Chapter Eleven

Silence woke him.

Sliding his hand over the sheets, Anthony reached out for her. Glimmers of green and pink illuminated the edges of the single window in his room. He rubbed his eyes with the ball of his palm. Damn, how long had he been asleep? Two hours? Three, tops? Time had lost all meaning once they'd finally climbed out of the shower. And he didn't regret a single moment, the feel of her wrapped around him still fresh in his mind. Her scent still clung to him. Being with her again… Hearing his name on her lips had been everything and so much more. He'd never forget tonight. And couldn't wait for so many others.

He rolled onto his side and scanned the bed with what minimal light came through the curtains. Empty. He narrowed his gaze to see through the dark. She couldn't have climbed out of bed that long ago. The sheets were still warm. "Glennon?"

A tingling sensation climbed up his spine.

The pressure of a gun barrel dug into his back. "Where is she?"

Anthony shot up and swung hard, knocking the weapon out of his assailant's hand. The thud of the gun hitting the floor resonated loudly in his ears.

Pain exploded across the right side of his head with a direct hit, but didn't slow him down. Grabbing his masked assailant by the back of the neck, he launched his knee into the attacker's stomach as hard as he could. No way in hell this bastard would get to her. He wouldn't fail her. Not again.

The intruder rammed his shoulder into Anthony's middle, shoving his bare feet across the cold hardwood floor. He slammed his elbow down into his opponent's spine. Once. Twice. His heart beat loudly behind his ears as the operative dropped—hard—but Anthony wasn't finished. Straddling his attacker, he rocketed his fist into the man's face. A knee caught him in the back and he launched forward, his head hitting the nightstand.

The intruder swung down, every move, every strike, militaristic.

Blocking the punch with one hand, Anthony rammed his fist into his assailant's rib cage. He shoved to his feet. A growl—predatory and full of rage—ripped from his throat as he closed in. These people just didn't get the message. Glennon Chase was off-limits. She was his. And he'd put a bullet in every single one of them to keep her safe.

A solid kick to the man's chest sent his opponent straight into the bedroom window. Broken glass rained down around them as his attacker slumped to the floor. But the fight was far from over. They'd already broken into his house twice, somehow bypassing his security. There wouldn't be a next time.

The bedroom light blinded him for a split second and he swung around, prepared for another fight.

Glennon stood in the doorway. Wearing nothing but one of his large T-shirts that covered her from mid-thigh up and her unlaced boots, her service weapon was firmly gripped between both hands. Standing there, unashamed and determined to do the job. And damn if that wasn't the sexiest thing he'd ever seen. Broken glass crunched under his attacker's boots as the bastard got to his feet. Glennon closed in on her target. Her gaze shifted to Anthony then back. Was that hesitation he read across her expression? "You know the drill, Bennett. Put your hands on your head and drop to your knees."

"You going to arrest me, Glennon?" The mask hid the intruder's features but that voice... Anthony recognized it straight off the bat. First from the break-in, then from the docks.

With slow movements, the attacker gripped the black ski mask in his hand and pulled it from his head. Brown hair and a sharp, shadowed jawline stood out against the hollowness that had consumed the sergeant's features. Running from the authorities had obviously taken a toll. "Here I thought we could still be friends after everything I've done for you."

Son of a bitch. They'd recovered Bennett Spencer. The investigation was over. His gaze cut back to Glennon. Anthony curled his fingers into his palms as a wall of heat rushed against him from the vent above his head. He'd gone to bed—and fought Bennett—in nothing but his boxers, but he wouldn't move a damn inch to get dressed as long as the bastard was free of cuffs.

"Done for me?" A rough laugh worked up her throat as Glennon shifted her weight to her back foot, widening her stance and making herself a smaller target, exactly as he'd taught her in basic. "You've got to be kidding. For two years, all you've done for me is lie. What you should be saying is, 'Thank you for not putting a bullet in me, Glennon.' Or 'Hey, partner, by the way, I'm part of the operation we've been tasked to investigate. Thought you should know.'"

"Well, I thought taking care of that sniper who put a bullet in your shoulder or saving your life at the side of the road was awful nice of me. I guess I could've let those assholes kill you." Bennett shrugged. The muscles along his jawline sharpened. Brown eyes—darker than coffee—locked on her, sending the controlled rage Anthony held on to close to the surface. "And, hey, partner, by the way, I'm not part of Mascaro's operation. At least…not anymore."

"What? Did they revoke your membership once

they found out you've been moonlighting as CID?" Glennon adjusted her grip on the gun. "And you're the one who ran us off the road in the first place. How am I supposed to trust anything you say?"

"You killed the sniper and that shooter on the shoreline." Anthony crossed to the closet and scanned his thumbprint for access to his gun safe. In another two, maybe three minutes, Glennon's arms would start to ache from holding her weapon up so long, but Bennett wouldn't get the drop on them. He loaded a magazine into his Beretta and secured a round in the chamber. Not again. This time he'd put the traitor down if forced. "If you were with Mascaro and his crew, why bother?"

"No offense, Ranger—" Bennett interlaced his hands behind his head "—but I think I'd be more comfortable having this conversation with all of us wearing clothes."

"No, we're doing this now, *partner.*" The last word sneered from Glennon's lips. She lowered her weapon but the rage etched into her features intensified. The safety on her gun remained off. She didn't trust Bennett. And with good reason. The sergeant had successfully infiltrated the Military Police—background checks, polygraph tests, multiple interviews. He'd lived a double life for years. Hell, if Bennett weren't part of the crew trying to kill the woman he loved, Anthony would have half a mind to recruit him into Blackhawk Security. "You betrayed the army. And me. In fact, I wouldn't be surprised if you're the one who deleted my files off my backup drive."

"Didn't I warn you not to come after me?" Bennett lowered his hands.

Anthony tightened his grip around the Beretta as the sergeant rose. One small move. That was all it would take and this entire recovery would be a thing of the past.

"Damn it, Bennett. Did you really think a warning would stop me from coming after you?" Tension tightened the tendon in Glennon's neck as she straightened. "Give me one good reason why I shouldn't arrest you right here, right now."

"You mean aside from the fact you don't have any proof I was part of Mascaro's operation? Come on, Glennon. You and I both know you'd be wasting your time. I'm a lot smarter than I look. Besides, we're on the same side. Mascaro's organization wants me dead as much as they want you. Maybe even more." Bennett studied her from head to toe, his expression cold. Calculating. Danger beneath smooth waters. A man who'd chosen treason over his country always had an escape plan in case things went south. So what was Bennett's? "What I can do is help you bring down Mascaro's crew for good. Interested?"

Confusion cracked Glennon's stone-cold control. "Why would you help us?"

"He's trying to avoid prison time." Anthony maneuvered between Glennon and her partner. He'd stand between her and any threat. Always. Not because they were partners in this investigation. But because it was her. "He wants to strike a deal with the new marshal when the investigation is over."

Couldn't blame him. If the army could connect Bennett with any of the crimes Mascaro and his operatives had been accused of, he'd never see the light of day again. A large part of Anthony reveled in that idea. Bennett had dragged Glennon—and her son—into this mess, had put her in the crosshairs. Then again, the sergeant had also saved her life. Twice.

A rumbling laugh escaped Bennett's throat. "I'm not going to prison, Ranger. Like I said, I'm smarter than I look." He crossed his muscled arms over his chest, shifting his weight between his feet. "Actually, I just plan to systematically kill every last one of those bastards. From the bottom hit man to the woman giving orders at the top."

Anthony's gaze focused on Bennett. Woman?

Glennon took a single step forward. Grip still wrapped around her weapon, she narrowed her gaze. "What woman?"

"Jamie Mascaro," Bennett said.

Anthony ran through Glennon's investigation notes in his head. "Staff Sergeant Mascaro's wife?"

"Bingo." Bennett uncrossed his arms, one hand facing toward Glennon and the other reaching for something in his leather jacket pocket. "And I've got the proof. Turns out she set her husband up from the beginning. She tipped the marshal off to the crew's extracurricular activities and put her husband front and center in our investigation. But then our CO decided to take a cut himself, but that's a story for another day." The sergeant offered Anthony a piece of paper, his attention cutting to Glennon as she maneuvered beside him. "She's a piece of work if you ask me. Kind of reminds me of you, Glennon. Only you're not evil."

"Let's say I believe you about being on Jamie Mascaro's bad side. You found out who'd taken Nicholas Mascaro's place at the head of the operation." Glennon studied the evidence as Anthony unfolded the beaten sheet of paper. "And that's the only reason they're hunting us down? Why you disappeared?"

A photo of a blonde woman—maybe thirty-five, forty years old—standing beside a military-marked crate, surrounded by soldiers, stared up at him. In her hands? An M4 assault rifle, same make and model of the shipment of missing weapons Glennon and Bennett had gone chasing in the first place. Jamie Mascaro. The woman most certainly knew of her husband's criminal activities, despite what her testimony had revealed during the staff sergeant's trial.

"Not exactly." Bennett tugged a hand through the gelled brown hair at the back of his neck. "That would be because I was one of Nicholas Mascaro's lieutenants. And Jamie there—" he nodded at the photo "—is cleaning house."

HER PARTNER HAD been one of Staff Sergeant Mascaro's men. Just as the marshal had claimed. Bennett had told them everything. How he'd faked his GPS data to draw out Jamie Mascaro to the abandoned house that belonged to her husband, how he'd waited there for the sniper who'd put a bullet in Glennon's shoulder then taken him out, and how he'd gotten through Anthony's security system at the cabin. Twice. All of it. Felony after felony stacked against the man she'd once considered her closest friend. Because this investigation couldn't get any worse.

Sweat lessened her grip on her Glock before she finally clicked on the safety and tossed it onto the bed. She'd just needed a minute to herself. Alone, Glennon dropped her head back against the bedroom door. Dark, rumpled sheets claimed her attention. She'd broken her only rule. She'd lost her emotional distance and fallen into bed with the one man she'd sworn to keep at arm's length. Yet at the same time Anthony had given her a glimpse of everything she'd ever wanted: a real family. A second chance.

Then Bennett had to ruin her short reprieve and everything else she'd believed the last few days. He was involved with the very people trying to kill her, but she couldn't prove it. Other than his admission, which she hadn't gotten on tape, he'd covered his tracks too well. But did she really want to? Bennett was the one man who could bring down Mascaro's crew for good. An insider. With his intel, they could disassemble the entire operation and secure weapons shipments all over the country. The investigation would be over. She could put in her discharge papers. She could move on with her life.

Glennon shoved away from the door, throwing her discarded clothing onto the bed.

A soft knock spun her around. "You okay?"

Anthony.

Her feet dragged as she headed to the door. Twisting the knob, she faced off with a wall of pure, seductive muscle. Dressed in a pair of low-hanging jeans and a black T-shirt, he was far sexier with his hair out of place and a little frightening with his hard, determined expression. She straightened a bit more, pressed her lips together and nodded once. "I'm fine."

A lie. What about the past three days had been fine? Hell, the last two hours had turned her entire world upside down. But he didn't need to know that. Her partner going missing hadn't broken her. Leaving her son hadn't broken her. Bennett's flat-out betrayal hadn't broken her. This thing with Anthony? That wouldn't break her, either.

Those deep, dark eyes narrowed on her. What did he see when he looked at her like that? How close she was to splintering apart? Could he see the cracks in her defenses widening? "You think I can't see it when you lie to me, but I do."

Heat climbed up her neck and into her face. Goose bumps rose on her arms as a blast of warm air descended from the vent in the ceiling. She cleared her throat. "What are you talking abou—?"

"You're already pulling away," he said.

"I meant what I said outside." Glennon swallowed hard as she leveled her chin parallel with the floor. "I won't have you come into my life—into my son's life—then disappear when you decide your duty is more important than we are."

"Is that what you think of me? That you're temporary? That I'll get bored? That this doesn't mean anything?" Growling, he closed in on her, fire replacing the cold depths in his eyes. "I took you to bed. No other woman can say the same. That means everything to me, Glennon. It means…you're mine."

His? Her breath caught. She forced her fingers to uncurl from her palms. He hadn't taken any other woman to bed? Ever? Warmth flooded her. She fought to think. To breathe. He was right. That did mean something. Her focus shifted to her engagement ring hanging around his neck. He'd never stopped believing they could be happy together.

"It meant something to me, too." The words left her mouth in a mere whisper as pain knifed through her. She'd learned a long time ago that those closest could turn on her in an instant. Her father. Bennett. Even Anthony had played an important role in building her defenses. And she wasn't sure she could survive that devastation again. She forced herself to take a step back when all she wanted was for him to wrap his arms around her. "But did you forget we've been through this before?"

His brows drew inward, tugging at the scrape across his forehead. His pulse beat unevenly at the base of his throat, eyelids heavier than a moment ago. Exhaustion pulled at his expression. Dirt still clung to his hairline. "We're not the same people we were back then. There's more at risk now. More reason to give us a shot."

Because of Hunter. Glennon exhaled hard. Her son had gone four years without a father in his life, someone other than her to count on. Anthony was right. They had a lot more to lose now. Maybe that was all they needed to finally make this work between them. She could, at last, give Hunter the real family he deserved. "Hunter and I… We're not some mission you can complete." She dragged her tongue across her lips, her mouth dry. "We need someone in it for the long haul."

"Have you ever known me as anything other than dedicated?" He lowered his mouth to hers but paused. "I dare you to find someone who loves you more than I do, sweetheart."

Her army-issue phone vibrated on the nightstand a few feet away.

The breath she'd been holding rushed from her lungs. Saved by the bell. Crossing the room, Glennon caught the number before one last ring. Blocked. She hit the green button and brought the phone to her ear. "Special Agent Chase—"

"I assume you know who I am," a female voice said.

Glennon turned to Anthony. Dropping the phone from her ear, she tapped the speaker button.

Confusion deepened the lines across his forehead as he inched closer.

"Jamie Mascaro." Glennon stared at the phone, ticking off the seconds on the screen. Thirty seconds. That was all she needed for Blackhawk Security to trace the call. Thirty seconds and she could end this nightmare. "Unless you're calling to apologize for sending three soldiers to kill me, I'm afraid we don't have a lot to talk about."

"Oh, I don't think that's true, Sergeant Chase." A light tapping sound echoed through the line. Fingernails on a desk? "See, you have something I want, a certain lieutenant from my husband's command who knows too much and puts my entire operation at risk. I was hoping you and I could make a deal. You turn Sergeant Spencer over to me and I'll call off the contract I put on your head."

Shadowed movement caught Glennon's attention in her peripheral vision. Bennett. Inhaling slow and deep, she motioned him inside. He was part of this, too. And while she could give him up—put an end to this investigation and move on with her life—there were still lines she wasn't willing to cross. Giving up her partner was one of them. No matter how much he might deserve it.

Tense moments ticked past. This was it. They could do this. Together. "Sorry to disappoint you, Mrs. Mascaro, but I don't make deals with crim—"

Laughter cut through her words. Sinister. Dominating. "Please, Sergeant Chase. Call me Jamie. Because, despite what you might think, we're about to become very well acquainted with one another. In fact, I'm willing to bet you'll do just about anything I ask once you uncover the small insurance policy I took out to secure your cooperation."

Insurance policy? Glennon searched Anthony's features. That full bottom lip, his dark blue eyes. Dread pooled at the base of her spine. Insurance—

"Mommy?" Hunter's voice crossed the line, draining the blood from her face.

Anthony swore, the small muscles lining his jaw rock-hard.

Her heart skipped a beat, the breath rushing from her lungs. Every muscle in her body threatened to fail. No. No, no, no, no. Her grip on the phone loosened as her knees buckled. The bedroom—and everyone in it—blurred. Rough hands caught her before she hit the floor, leading her to the edge of the bed. The mattress dipped with Anthony's added weight.

Her throat tightened. "Hunter?" She swallowed hard, closing her eyes. "Is that you?"

"Mommy, I want to go home." The desperation in her son's small voice gutted her.

Rage, white and hot, flooded through her. She opened her eyes. Her vision sharpened. She clung to the phone. Fifteen more seconds. Fifteen more seconds and she'd have a location. Forget bringing Anthony as backup. Glennon would rip the woman apart with her bare hands. "I'm coming, baby. I promise. Mommy is coming for you."

No answer.

"Hunter?" Panic threatened to set in. Had Mascaro hung up? The timer on the screen read twenty seconds. Not enough time to trace the call. Glennon nearly shattered the phone, her pulse too loud in her ears.

"Such a sweet little boy. It'd be a shame if he didn't come home," Jamie Mascaro said. "You know what I want, Sergeant Chase, and I know you're tracing this call. All you have to do is bring me Sergeant Spencer and I will disclose your son's location. You have my word."

The word of a criminal, a woman who'd turned on her own husband to take over his operation.

Glennon studied Bennett. Deep brown eyes, darker than a few minutes ago, softened. His nod released the pressure in her chest. He'd turn himself over to Jamie Mascaro. For her. For Hunter. "If

I find a single bruise on him when I find him, I will kill you."

"That will be entirely up to you, Sergeant," Jamie Mascaro said. "Two hours. Come alone with Sergeant Spencer or your son pays the price."

The line went dead.

"Well, this seems like a good time to give you two some privacy. And, you know, get my affairs in order before that woman puts a bullet in my head." Bennett headed into the hallway, the jokes, the witty banter, his sarcasm, draining from his expression.

Glennon tossed the phone onto the bed, numb. Jamie Mascaro had her son. Her hands shook, blood pressure dropping fast. Tears burned on her lower eyelashes a split second before another rush of fury swept through her. She ripped the bedside lamp off the table and hurled it at the wall. This was why she'd kept her son a secret. Why she hadn't told his father about him. She forced her focus to Anthony. Helplessness threatened to consume her. She had to stay in the moment, stay in control. The second she gave in to those thoughts, Jamie Mascaro—and her organization of traitorous thieves—won. Running her palms down her bare thighs, Glennon rolled her lips between her teeth to keep from screaming. "She's not going to hold up her end of the deal."

She was sure of it.

"Then we've got two hours to find Hunter before the meeting." The words came as a growl from

Anthony's throat. The veins in his arms swelled. Pure ice squelched the fire that had simmered in his gaze a moment ago, all evidence of the man she'd started falling in love with gone. The Grim Reaper had arrived, but this time, she wouldn't try to hold him back. "I swear to you, I'll get your son back."

"Good." Glennon straightened. She had to tell him. If they were going to risk it all—if they were going to recover Hunter—she couldn't lie to him anymore. She cleared her throat. "Because Hunter is your son, too."

Chapter Twelve

There were only two things in life a person couldn't take back. Bullets and words. The latter stuck with him now. *Because Hunter is your son, too.* She'd kept his son from him for four damn years. The little boy with the bright green eyes and wide smile. She'd kept his family from him. Rage exploded in his chest. But he couldn't think about that right now. Not with Hunter out there. Afraid. In danger. Alone.

"Don't think we're finished talking about this." Anthony strode across the street toward her childhood home for the second time in twenty-four hours. No way in hell were they finished. In fact, they were just getting started.

"Fine. You want to talk about this right now, with our son missing?" Glennon spun on her heel, shoving a hand against his chest in the middle of the street. Arctic temperatures formed crystalized puffs of air in front of her mouth, but the cold barely seemed to slow her down. "Yes, I kept him from you, just like I kept him from everyone else. I didn't want the people I hunted for the military to ever have leverage over me, but apparently, everything I've done to keep him safe has all been for nothing. They found him. He's out there—" tears welled in her eyes as she motioned toward the street "—all alone. Because of me."

"I could've protected him, Glennon. I could've prevented this from happening if you'd just told me the truth." Devastation deepened the lines forged between her eyebrows, and his gut tightened. She blamed herself for this mess, but she wasn't innocent. His fury burned hot and deep. First, she'd kept evidence crucial to identifying a suspect to herself. Second, kept the break in at her apartment back east from him. Now this. Jamie Mascaro would pay for what she'd done, but how was he supposed to trust Glennon now? Closing his fingers around her arms, Anthony forced her to look at him. "I'm only going to say this once, and I want you to believe every word. None of this—Bennett disappearing, the bullet in your shoulder, the accident, Hunter being kidnapped—is your fault. That's on Jamie Mascaro, and she's going to pay for the rest of her life. I'm going to make sure of it, but I can't do my damn job when you're keeping things from me."

"I should've been there for him." The words were whispered from between her paling lips as though she hadn't heard a single word he'd said. "I should've been the one keeping him safe. Maybe then, this wouldn't have happened."

"You were. You did everything in your power to make sure he couldn't be connected to you." He couldn't keep this space between them any longer. Wrapping her in his arms, Anthony rested his chin on the crown of her head. She fit perfectly, almost as though they were two pieces of the same puzzle.

Alaskan temperatures battled with her natural heat. He memorized the feel of her pressed against him all over again. The rise and fall of her shoulders intensified the friction between them. He had to concentrate on the operation—on getting his son back—and not the fact she'd lied to him for close to five years. "Jamie Mascaro outmaneuvered us this time. It won't happen again."

"Well, I wish that made me feel better." Pulling back slightly, she wiped at her eyes. Strands of hair escaped from the tight braid at the back of her head, all evidence of the controlled, emotionally distant investigator a distant memory. Love did that sometimes, had a way of breaking even the strongest person in two, and he had no doubt in that moment: Glennon was breaking. "The meeting is in a couple hours, and I doubt Bennett will wait back at the cabin much longer. We need to get moving."

"We're going to get our son back, Glennon, and, after we do, you and I are going to finish this conversation," he said.

She nodded. Twisting around, she headed toward the house. Then froze. She drew her service weapon at the sight of the busted front door, rushing forward. "Mom?"

"No." Anthony caught her by the arm and pulled her back, then unholstered his Beretta. He trusted his instincts. Jamie Mascaro already had what she wanted: leverage. The new head of her husband's operation didn't have any reason to leave operatives behind, but he wasn't going to risk Glennon going inside without him surveying the property first. He nodded to the west side of the house. There'd always been a chance Helen Chase would become a target, but he honestly prayed for the operatives who tried to take her out. "Get behind me."

She maneuvered into position, gun in hand, close on his heels.

He led them around the back of the house, senses on high alert. Snow crunched under his boots as he spotted a path of three distinct sets of footprints. Anthony raised his left hand, signaling for Glennon to stop. Three-man team. Their tracks headed toward the front of the house, originating from the tree line. The perfect approach, seeing as how there weren't any windows on this side of the house. Helen never would've seen them coming. However, one set had deviated from formation, forging a path to the breaker box. He crouched near the box and picked up a severed padlock.

"What is it?" Moonlight cast Glennon's shadow over his shoulder.

"They cut the power to the house." He tossed the padlock back into the snow. "And to Helen's alarm system." He straightened. These bastards had taken his son. Orders be damned, he'd make them pay. But first, they had to get to Helen. She was the only one who might be able to give them a lead on where Mascaro had taken his son. "Let's go."

They cleared the backyard. No movement. No sign of an impending ambush. Testing the back-door screen, Anthony reached for one of the blades tucked into his arsenal and cut through the aluminum mesh. The door was secure. If they played their cards right, there wouldn't be reason for anyone still inside to think it wasn't secure. They could surprise these bastards, finally gain the upper hand. And maybe secure some leverage of their own.

"Wait." Glennon reached over him and into the light fixture to his right. A moment later she handed him a key. He stared down at her but she only shrugged. "My mother hid a spare key out here in case one of my friends needed a place to stay. Guess she forgot about it."

Anthony inserted the key into the lock and twisted the doorknob. Letting his Beretta lead, he shouldered his way inside. He fought to adjust to the darkness. One. Two. Three seconds was all the time he needed before ice ran through his veins. The house had been destroyed, every inch littered with debris, bullet casings, glass. And blood.

A sharp gasp reached his ears from behind. Glennon.

His grip tightened on the gun. Damn it, he shouldn't have brought her in here. She'd already lost her son. Who knew what else they were about to find. If Mascaro's people had laid a hand on Helen, they'd wish they had killed him back in that parking garage. They had to find her. Fast, Anthony nodded toward the living room. The team had come through the front door, straight into the living room. If they were going to find anything—anyone—it'd be there.

Following the trail of debris through the kitchen, he slowed his movements so as not to shift the evidence. The second they secured Helen, he'd call in Vincent Kalani. Blackhawk's forensic expert would lead them to the men responsible for this mess, and Anthony would take it from there.

Moonlight highlighted the origin of the battle. Bookcases overturned. Sofas losing their cushioning through bullet holes. The coffee table tipped on its side. The space had transformed into the complete opposite of his last memories in this room. Memories of Hunter.

Movement claimed his attention on the left.

A shotgun blast exploded from the darkness. Arcing wide, it barely missed his right arm.

Anthony pulled Glennon to the floor with him,

ready for another shot. Hiking his weapon up and over his head, he aimed for the shooter taking cover behind the last remaining bookcase. His ears rang. His heart beat hard at the back of his skull. Next chance he got, he'd take the shot.

"No, don't shoot!" Glennon climbed over his legs and wrapped one hand around his wrist. Her breath fanned across his neck, raising goose bumps along his overheated skin. "Mom, it's okay. It's me. It's Glennon."

Shadows shifted behind the bookcase. "They took him." Flat, strained words. "I did everything I could. I shot one of them. But the other two…they…took him right out of my arms."

Relief flooded through him. Helen was alive. Shoving to his feet, Anthony lowered his weapon as Glennon rushed to her mother. He scanned the rest of the living room. Television destroyed. Area rug covered in glass and…a blue blanket decorated with monsters. Stained with blood.

The sound of glass shifting across the hardwood floor broke through the silence from behind him. Every muscle in his body tensed. They weren't alone. One of Mascaro's operatives had stayed behind after all. His fingers tightened around the gun. He spun on his heel.

"Anthony?" Glennon helped her mother into a nearby chair.

Closing the distance, Anthony caught sight of one

of the intruders fighting to crawl to the safety of the front door. Not a chance in hell. He lunged for the operative. Gripping the man's Kevlar, Anthony forced the bastard to his feet and slammed him into the nearest wall. A groan escaped the guy's throat. Rage boiled beneath Anthony's skin. The edges of his vision darkened, focusing on his prey. "Where did they take him?"

A white smile disrupted the smear of blood across the soldier's face. No answer.

Pulling the intruder toward him, he placed the barrel of his gun under the guy's chin and clicked off the Beretta's safety. "Where?"

"Anthony." Glennon rushed into his peripheral vision. But she wouldn't be able to talk him down. Not this time.

Blood dripped onto his boots. Helen had been right. She'd hit the bastard all right. And Anthony would let him bleed out in the middle of the entry-way if the son of a bitch didn't start talking soon.

Glennon approached slowly, her service weapon aimed. "This one's mine."

ONE SHOT. That was all it had taken to get Hunter's location out of the shooter. And with a single call to Bennett, they finally had the upper hand. They were going to end this nightmare once and for all.

Anthony shoved the SUV into Park along the dirt road. "We're here."

"Good." This was it. Up ahead, a small wooden shed sat in the middle of dried weeds and tall dead trees off to the left. The sun had gone down, but clear tire tracks dug uneven paths along the road. For an abandoned water shed, the area had obviously been used recently. Anticipation surged through her. According to Mascaro's man, her son was being held in that shed until further instruction. This could all be over in a few minutes.

But...

She checked the burner phone Anthony had supplied, rolling her lips between her teeth.

"No word from Bennett. He should've been here by now." Had he changed his mind about turning himself over to Mascaro? Her rib cage tightened. Glennon leaned forward in her seat, fingernails digging into the soft leather. They'd parked a few hundred feet from the shed, but even from this distance there should've been some evidence Hunter was in that building. Lights. Guards. Cameras. Vehicles. And where the hell was Bennett? Dread pooled in her stomach. This was wrong. It was too quiet. "This doesn't feel right. Bennett should be here by now."

"It's a trap." Anthony's voice dipped an octave. Gaze cutting to the rearview mirror, he reached for his weapon. "Get down!"

The back window shattered.

Glennon launched forward. A flash grenade landed in the back seat and she rushed to cover her ears. In vain. Her vision brightened into nothing but white as an explosion robbed her of her hearing. Pings of sound registered through the ringing in her ears. Gunshots? She couldn't be sure, feeling blindly for the weapon she'd dropped onto the floor.

A blast of Alaskan air rushed against her a split second before rough hands pulled her from the SUV. Snow and dead weeds crunched beneath her as she hit the ground. Muted voices echoed around her as she was wrenched to her feet and pushed forward. She tumbled into the side of the SUV, the grenade affecting her balance. She blinked to clear her vision. Two seconds. Three. Shadows shifted in front of her but she couldn't make them out. "Where is my son?"

Another push.

She landed on all fours, rocks and ice cutting into her palms. Her vision cleared in small increments, revealing five armed operatives in front of her, but a flash of headlights kept their identities shadowed. The ringing in her ears lessened as another soldier zip-tied her wrists behind her back. Pain splintered across her wounded shoulder, eliciting a groan from her throat, and she clamped down hard on her back teeth.

Anthony landed on his knees beside her, the stain of blood thick in his hairline.

She fought against the zip ties. "Anthony—"

"Grab Hunter as soon as you can and run. Don't worry about me." His voice leveled out. Deep. Dark.

Dangerous. Where fire usually blazed in his blue eyes, coldness stared back at her and her breath caught.

"Sergeant Chase, I thought I made myself perfectly clear." A woman, presumably Jamie Mascaro, stepped around one of the vehicles and in front of the headlights. Her heeled boots wobbled on the uneven terrain, long hair shifting over her shoulder. "You were to bring me Sergeant Spencer at the designated meeting point alone."

"Where is he? Where is my son?" Plastic cut deep into her wrists the more she struggled, but she wouldn't stop. Wouldn't give in.

Jamie Mascaro stepped forward. "You broke our deal—"

"Where is he!" Glennon lunged to her feet, but a hand on her injured shoulder shoved her back to her knees.

A predatory growl reached her ears a split second before Anthony twisted around. A flash of metal caught her eye as the operative holding him collapsed. Unconscious or dead, she didn't know. Did it matter? Headlights highlighted the thin layer of sweat on Anthony's cheeks, his expression perfectly cold. Perfectly dangerous. A single step toward her raised goose bumps along her neck and arms. "Get your damn hands off her or wind up like your friend here."

The soldier backed off.

Her throat dried on her next inhale. Wrenching away from the grip on her shoulder, she left the soldier at her back to fend for himself as Jamie Mascaro signaled for the other four armed men to stand down. The zip ties fell to the ground with a swipe of Anthony's blade. Glennon fought the urge to rub at the raw skin, collected the assault rifle at her feet and aimed for Jamie Mascaro. "You have five seconds to bring me my son, or I give the signal for Sergeant Spencer to put a bullet in your head."

Such a lie. Bennett wasn't a sniper and she still hadn't heard from him, but she had to try something. She had no doubt Anthony could take down a couple of Jamie Mascaro's operatives, but the two of them against five armed men with assault rifles? Not a chance. She needed to see Hunter. Make sure he was okay. She could figure out the rest later.

"You think I didn't know about your little reconnaissance mission?" A high-pitched laugh drifted across the dirt. Jamie Mascaro angled her head over her shoulder, nodding once. A soldier to her left circled around one of the vehicles and reached inside, extracting a zip-tied man from the back seat.

Glennon narrowed her gaze, her fingers tightening around the gun's stock. The man's size, stature, even his walk, revealed his identity before the headlights did. Restrained, bruised and bloodied, he stared straight at her through swollen eyelids as her stomach flipped. "Bennett."

They'd captured him. The investigation against Mascaro's operation, the evidence, all of it depended on him. Without Bennett, she couldn't close this case. Without him…she had nothing. Jamie Mascaro was going to kill him, and the army would be forced to drop the investigation. She'd walk free. But then why was Jamie Mascaro still here? She had what she wanted.

The gunman shoved Bennett down onto his knees.

"Move." Anthony pushed the operative behind her forward. Dust clouded the streak of headlights shining on them, but she caught sight of the blade at the soldier's throat clearly. "You have three seconds to bring out the boy or I start gutting your men one by one."

Another laugh reached her ears. Jamie Mascaro hiked a hand to her waist. "Oh, I like you. Need a job, Ranger? The pay is phenomenal."

Glennon shifted her weight between her feet. Coldness worked down into her bones. The snake already had what she wanted. What more could she—

The realization hit hard, the air rushing from her lungs as though she'd taken a punch to the stomach. Ice worked through her. Jamie Mascaro wasn't just after Bennett Spencer. The new head of the operation wanted more. "We had a deal."

"One," Anthony said.

"A deal that you broke, Sergeant Chase. Granted, I planned on breaking it to begin with, but you beat me to the punch. Now we're going to strike a new deal. One you won't be able to back out of." The woman came closer, balancing on those impractical heeled boots. High-arched eyebrows, thin lips and piercing eyes came into focus. "Bring out the boy."

Every muscle along Glennon's spine tensed. She swallowed back the tightness in her throat. Seconds passed. A full minute. She scanned the ring of vehicles, covering the glare of headlights with one hand as she squinted past the brightness. Where was he?

Anthony stilled, waiting, with the soldier still struggling in his grip. But the bastard was no match for her Ranger. No one was.

A small outline rushed from between the vehicles but was held back by one of Jamie Mascaro's men. "Mommy!"

"Hunter." Glennon took a step forward, ready to risk going up against assault rifles and the men carrying them to get to him. She dropped the gun to her side. He didn't need to see her holding a weapon. He was scared enough. "I'm here, baby. This will all be over soon."

"Let go!" The four-year-old swiped at the soldier holding on to him, but the hits didn't faze Mascaro's man.

Hers would. And the second she had the chance, she'd take every single one of them out.

"You're right. This will all be over soon." Jamie Mascaro raised a gun of her own, a small Ruger she'd hidden in her coat pocket, and aimed. At Anthony. "But not for you, Sergeant Chase. I want to get to know you better."

With a direct hit to the soldier in his hold, Anthony knocked the operative unconscious.

Glennon's heart worked to explode out of her chest.

Anthony discarded his hostage into the snow, and stepped between her and Jamie Mascaro. Always the protector. Always putting her first. "You're out of your damn mind if you think a bullet from you will stop me from getting to that boy."

Nausea rolled through her. Then rage. Hell no, it wouldn't. Anthony would fight until the job was finished, bullet wounds be damned. But... She couldn't lose him. Not again. "You want Sergeant Spencer in exchange for my son—" she took a deep, cleansing breath, Mascaro's intentions crystal-clear now "—and you want me in exchange for Sergeant Major Harris."

The weight of Anthony's wide gaze compressed the air in her lungs. "Not happening."

"You're one of the few people who know who I am." Jamie Mascaro held the Ruger steady. "And I can't have you running around revealing my identity. If word got out who was running my husband's operation..." She cocked her head to one side. "Let's just say I worked too long and too hard to overthrow Nicholas to lose allies because I'm a woman."

Sweat dripped down Glennon's spine. Her mouth dried. "The deal you made. It was a setup from the beginning. You weren't ever planning on letting me go home with my son."

"Well, I am a criminal, Sergeant Chase. You had to see it coming," Mascaro said.

Hunter for Bennett. Anthony for her. Glennon straightened a bit more. Judging by the way the woman's hand shook holding the gun up for this long, she could take out Jamie Mascaro, no problem. The woman wasn't a soldier. She'd just taken control of her husband's criminal organization. Glennon would be cutting off the head of the snake. But... Her shoulders sank. There was no guarantee Mascaro's men wouldn't follow through with their orders. That left Anthony, Bennett and Hunter all at risk. A risk she couldn't afford.

"Glennon," Anthony said, "don't even think about it. We'll find another way."

He could always read her. That was what made him so damn good at his job. She focused on Hunter struggling to get free of the armed soldier behind him, then memorized everything she could about the operative. When she had the chance, she'd make him pay for putting his hands on her son.

There was no other way. At least, not one that would get Hunter home tonight. And as for Anthony... Glennon tossed the weapon she'd lifted off the soldier into the snow. She wouldn't lose him again. Not like this. "You've done the job I hired you for, sweetheart, but I'm assigning you a new one." A faint smile curled her lips. When would be the next time he called her that? Her throat threatened to close as she raised her hands over her head in surrender to Jamie Mascaro.

"Take care of our son."

Chapter Thirteen

She was tearing him apart.

"You're not doing this." Anthony wrapped his hand around her arm, jerking her into him. Like hell his job was finished. Did she honestly think he'd let her walk away again? After everything they'd been through? They had a son together. His muscles ached from tension, every cell in his body ready to rip these bastards apart with his bare hands. Only he couldn't. Not with a chance of Hunter getting caught in the crosshairs. He unclenched his jaw. "I won't lose you again."

"You're running out of time, Sergeant Chase," Jamie Mascaro said.

Four operatives left, each armed with an M4 assault rifle. Plus Jamie Mascaro and her Ruger. Any one of those bullets could rip apart his life. Anthony tightened his grip on the gun he'd taken from the bastard who'd dared put his hands on Glennon. The knife wouldn't do a damn bit of good. Six rounds.

Five targets. His attention slid to Hunter. One innocent, perfect, four-year-old boy. Didn't leave a whole lot of room for error.

"You're not losing me." She framed his jawline with her hands, brilliant green eyes locked on him. A rush of her rosy scent drove straight into his lungs. "Besides, you're not the only one trained in combat, Ranger. I know how to take care of myself."

Yet she'd offered herself up as the perfect hostage.

Rage rode him hard, but he tried to hold it back. For her. For Hunter. "I can do this. Say the word and I'll—"

Glennon fastened her hands behind his neck and pulled him against her. His mouth crashed onto hers. Ferocious desire exploded through him, igniting his strongest protective instincts. Having her to himself these last three days… It wasn't enough. It would never be enough. She had worked herself under his skin, and he had no idea how to get her out. Didn't want to know how. Her hands slid against his cheek. So soft. So…final.

Pulling away from him, Glennon set her forehead against his. "Protect Hunter. No matter what."

"Enough." Jamie Mascaro's voice penetrated the haze clouding his mind. Two soldiers came forward and ripped Glennon out of his hold. "I'm running out of patience."

His fingers burned against the dropping temperatures and the freezing steel of the rifle in his hand.

Anthony took a single step forward, fire raging in his veins, but two more assault rifle barrels promised to cut him down if given the chance. He couldn't help her. Couldn't save her. But he could save their son. "This isn't over, Mascaro. Doesn't matter where you hide, I'm coming for you."

"I look forward to it, Ranger. But remember. I saved your life today. I could've killed you anytime and you wouldn't have seen it coming." Jamie Mascaro turned her back on him with a nod to the operative holding onto his son. "Shoot Sergeant Major Harris if he moves an inch." She paused. "Better yet. Shoot *her* if he moves an inch."

"Mommy!" Hunter ran through the snow, wrapping his arms around his mother's legs, and Anthony's gut clenched. "Where are you going?"

"Stay with Anthony, baby." Glennon didn't have the chance to stop as the two operatives at her side pulled her toward the waiting vehicles, leaving Hunter in the snow. Alone.

Anthony fanned his grip over the gun in his hand. He couldn't take a step. Not without igniting an all-out war. Her footsteps wavered as they led her to one of the SUVs. December flakes disrupted the blinding light coming from the headlights, but the heartbreak in her last words was clear. She didn't believe she was coming home. Her voice strained as she looked back over her shoulder. "He's going to watch over you until I can come home, okay?"

Another soldier wrenched Bennett to his feet and hurled him back inside one of the waiting vehicles. Separate from his partner.

Anthony tried to get his control back, but Glennon had been the only one who could talk him down from the brink of rage. Always had been. His heart beat too loud, the rush of adrenaline too strong. He gripped the gun hard. He had to focus. Breathe. But every breath pressurized in his lungs.

He had to get her back. He *would* get her back. But not right now.

He watched as Glennon ripped herself out of the soldiers' holds, determined to walk on her own. She'd let this play out, but on her terms. Despite the fact she was walking away from him—again—Anthony had to respect her for that. Two gunmen collected their unconscious soldiers from the snow a few feet away, loading them into one of the SUVs.

Engines growled to life as Glennon paused, her gaze locking on his. A single nod was all she gave him before ducking inside the waiting vehicle, Jamie Mascaro close behind. In thirty seconds, the road was clear, snowflakes dimming distant taillights.

She was gone.

"Hunter." Anthony dropped the rifle and rushed forward, sliding onto his knees as he wrapped his arms around the boy. Cold worked through his clothing and deep into his bones. He lifted Hunter against him. "It's okay. I've got you. You're safe."

His son shook in his arms. "Where's Mommy going?"

"She'll be right back." Anthony stared after the disappearing convoy. Spinning back toward his SUV, he hung on to Hunter with everything he had. "I promise."

He wrenched the back door open, tossing the remains of the flash grenade into the snow. After securing his son in the seat, he pulled his emergency kit from the hidden compartment in the floor.

Anthony exhaled hard. His son. Hell, he had a son. He still couldn't believe Glennon had kept Hunter from him.

He wrapped his son in the blanket from his kit, pure green eyes—the same shade as Glennon's—staring up at him. Running his hand through the boy's short blond hair, he curled his hand around the back of Hunter's neck. No more mistakes. No distractions. Glennon was coming home. But first he had to get Hunter to safety. He extracted the burner phone stashed under the extra ammunition and hit the speed dial for Blackhawk Security.

The line rang only once.

"Oh, good. You're alive." Sullivan Bishop's voice pulled the logistical side of his mind onto the next operation: recovering Glennon Chase. "I was beginning to wonder."

"Glennon's been taken," he said.

"Give me the details." Two snapping sounds

crossed the line. Sullivan most likely trying to get the team's attention. "Location?"

"Five operators, plus the leader, all armed with M4s. All military. I'm one mile southwest outside Far North Bicentennial Park. Track my vehicle's GPS for an exact location." He checked his watch. Anthony studied the small shed off the side of the road. "Bogies on the move two minutes and counting, headed north. One civilian left behind." His gaze cut to Hunter huddled in the blanket, drifting off to sleep. His son was safe. That was all that mattered. His jaw hung open, heart rate dropping as adrenaline drained from his veins. "Send whoever you've got. Now."

"We have your location. Elizabeth, Vincent and Elliot are wheels-up in two," Sullivan said. "ETA fifteen minutes."

His grip tightened around the phone, the plastic protesting. Fifteen minutes. Too long. Every minute he wasted waiting around for backup, the greater the chance he'd lose the convoy's tracks. Anthony forced his tongue from the top of his mouth. But he wasn't about to put Hunter in danger. The boy had been through enough. First being taken from his grandmother by force, then losing his mother.

He didn't have a choice. He had to wait.

"Hold on a second." Sullivan's end of the line went silent. Two seconds. Three. In less than two minutes, Glennon could be anywhere in Anchorage. Jamie

Mascaro had the resources and the contacts to get a private plane out of the state in under an hour. They had to make a move. Now. "Vincent had his contact in Anchorage PD forward the forensics report from the scene at Helen Chase's home."

Anticipation flooded through him. "And?"

"The shooter's boots had a specific gravel stuck in the treads, and we were able to track it to a stretch of warehouses near Tina Lake. The system matched it instantly to the manufacturer, thanks to an unsolved robbery from last year. Could be a lead on your girl," Sullivan said. "And don't think we aren't going to talk about the bullet in that guy's leg. It's only a matter of time before Anchorage PD gets a hit on the ballistics."

The bastard was lucky one bullet was all Glennon had had the stomach for, considering he'd helped Jamie Mascaro kidnap her son.

"Is the shooter talking?" The warehouse theory was all they had, but he wasn't about to go in blind. Too many risks. Too many ways the entire operation could go sideways. Too many ways he could lose Glennon for good. "Anything I can use?"

"No." Sullivan lowered his voice. "Listen, Anchorage PD is collecting a lot of bodies linked to this investigation. They can't charge you with anything yet, but, Anthony, I've been there. I know exactly what you're thinking."

Sullivan had been there. One month ago when his

own brother had come back from the dead to target Captain Jane Reise, Sullivan's then-client and now the love of his life. The former SEAL had shot his own flesh and blood to save the woman he loved. Something Anthony was more than prepared to do for Glennon. "So promise me whatever happens when the Grim Reaper comes calling, it'll be clean. For your own good and mine."

Anthony stared into the fresh tracks at his feet. If it hadn't been for Sullivan, he would've been left for dead in Afghanistan during his last mission for the Rangers. He owed the former SEAL his life. But no matter how much he wanted to give his word, to promise this wouldn't come back onto Blackhawk Security and his team, he couldn't. Jamie Mascaro was about to find out exactly what kind of monster Anthony had caged all these years.

"Redirect the team. Have them meet me at Tina Lake." He hung up then dropped the phone into the snow, crushing it under his boot. Wrenching open the driver's-side door, he hurried in behind the wheel. The engine growled to life and he shoved the SUV into Drive. He hiked himself higher in the seat to get a better view of the back seat, of his son. The boy stared sleepily back at him. Anthony took a deep breath. No question. Just as Sullivan had been given the choice, he'd do whatever it took to recover the love of his life. Forget duty. Forget why she'd hired him in the first place. He wasn't going anywhere. Not without Glennon.

"Let's go get your mom, buddy."

GLENNON OPENED HER EYES, gasping. Clarity came in a sudden, sharp rush. Ice squeezed her body as she fought against the zip ties at her wrists and ankles. Her head pounded. What the hell had Mascaro drugged her with? She brought her bound hands to her neck, wincing, cold seeping into her clothing. The injection site burned. The convoy had gone maybe a mile from the abandoned water shed when she'd been drugged. She could be anywhere right now. Shaking off the gripping effects of the drug, she focused on the only source of warmth pressed against one side of her.

Bennett?

His shoulders rose and fell in even currents. He was alive—breathing—but had most likely been drugged with the same cocktail. She blinked against the pain tightening the muscles down the back of her neck. She had to focus. Make a plan. Because she wasn't dying today. Not when she'd gotten her son back. Not when she'd gotten Anthony back. She shifted on the cold cement floor. They had to get out of here. Glennon studied the massive empty space. Wherever here was. "Bennett, wake up."

Shoving against her partner, she sat up. A wave of dizziness closed in fast, but she kept her balance.

Barely. She uncurled her stiff fingers. Had Jamie Mascaro really stripped them of their coats? Reaching for her boots, she untied her shoelaces then tied them together through the ties at her wrists. She'd never had to saw her way through zip ties before, but there was a first time for everything. Seesawing her feet back and forth, she worked through the plastic. The muscles down her thighs burned, her body heavy.

Movement registered to her left. Lights flared from around a closed door. Someone was coming. She worked faster, harder. Mascaro had made her intentions perfectly clear. She and Bennett were to be interrogated then dealt with. Killed.

The ties at her wrists snapped, but she still had to deal with her ankles. And her partner. "Bennett."

A deep groan reached her ears. "Why does it feel like someone hit me over the head?"

"If you don't get yourself out of those zip ties, you're going to have a much bigger headache when Jamie Mascaro puts a bullet between your eyes." She inhaled long and deep, forcing her heart rate to slow. Concentrate.

"Why, Glennon, is that you?" Pain roughened his voice. Bennett struggled to sit up, his boots scraping against the cold cement floor. The light from around the door reflected off the whites of his eyes, but it was still too dark to make out anything other than a few old haul trucks. "Last thing I remember is someone sticking a needle in my neck while I was scouting out the location. Did we win?"

"Not yet." Her hands shook. She balled them into fists and stretched her knees out to opposite sides. With one strong push on either knee, the zip tie around her ankles snapped. She bit back a moan as the plastic cut into her briefly, then pushed to her feet. "Mascaro changed the rules. She exchanged Hunter for you. Then Anthony's life for mine."

A laugh rumbled from Bennett's chest as she crouched beside him to help him sit straight. "And here I thought the woman who wants me dead would stick to her word. Shame on me."

"And here I thought I could trust my partner. Shame on me." The words left her mouth much sharper than she'd intended. But there were some sins that couldn't be wiped clean with a joint abduction.

Glennon unlaced his boots and retied them as she'd done with hers. The ties snapped after a full minute of·silence. He could take care of his ankles himself. Standing, she surveyed the space. A warehouse of some kind. Moisture clung to the air, dampening her clothing more than the sweat working down her collarbone. A warehouse near water. Lake or Pacific Ocean? Only one way to find out.

"Glennon, wait." Bennett straightened, his dark outline wobbling toward her before his strength returned. The dizziness. Whatever Jamie Mascaro had drugged them with clung tight to their nervous systems. Who knew how long it would pull them down? "I need you to know why I did it. Why I joined Nicholas Mascaro's crew. It wasn't for the money, although it was a nice perk."

"I don't think now is a good time." She ran her sweaty palms down her jeans, searching for another door in the barren space. Too dark. They'd have to spread out. Fast. Before the guys with guns came back.

"We're not being shot at yet," Bennett said. "I think now is the perfect time."

Something in her snapped. What was it with the men in her life determined to talk things through at the most inconvenient times? He wanted to talk about this now? With Jamie Mascaro and her traitorous soldiers right outside the door? Fine. Her face heated then went ice-cold. "It doesn't matter why you did it, Bennett. You lied to me. You betrayed me and this country. I let you into my life, into my son's life. I trusted you and you threw it in my face—"

"Nicholas Mascaro was a witness in my sister's disappearance." Bennett ran a shadowed hand over his face. "He saw the suspect two minutes before she vanished off base."

What? Her stomach sank. The American flag pin. She'd known it had belonged to his sister, but the reason he'd held on to it… Damn. Losing someone that close, someone you loved more than anything, would change anyone. For better or for worse. Anthony's pale features as he lost blood due to his wounds in the parking garage flashed across her mind. She couldn't imagine that pain. Didn't want to imagine it.

Glennon swallowed hard, her throat closing. "I'm sorry. I didn't… You never said anything."

"Well, it's not exactly something I advertise, seeing as how she's the reason I chose to betray my country. And my partner." He tapped his knuckles into her arm. "Nicholas brought me into the operation to help find her abductor. Made me a lieutenant to gain the trust of his contacts and use them to track down the man who…" A shaky inhale reached her ears through the darkness. "The guy might've been the head of a criminal organization, but he was the only lead I had. In return, I got him access to the big guns on base. Before I knew it, I was embedded deeper than I intended. Guess his wife doesn't like that."

"Did you find him? The man who took your sister?" Glennon ran her hands along the nearest wall, searching for anything that could get them outside. Ten seconds passed. Twenty. The hairs on the back of her neck stood on end. Every cell in her body waited in anticipation as Bennett searched the other side of the room.

"No, I never found him." His voice lightened as he maneuvered past her toward another wall. "And I never will if we don't get the hell out of here."

Right. Glennon shook off the tightness in her

chest, staring after his retreating form. Jamie Mascaro wasn't going to wait around for them to make up before she put a bullet in their heads. But one thing was clear. "I would've done the same thing, you know."

Bennett froze mid-escape. "Done what, exactly?"

"If I'd lost the one person I loved more than anyone in the world like that, I would've done whatever I had to, to find whoever had taken them from me." She took a step forward. The image of Anthony rushing toward her son out the back window of the SUV—their son—after she'd surrendered herself had burned itself into her mind. It was that exact moment when she'd realized what she was losing by getting into the back seat of the SUV with Jamie Mascaro: her family.

No matter how hard she'd fought to keep him at arm's length, no matter how many times she'd tried to convince herself he'd leave when duty called, her Ranger had worked his way back into her heart. She'd fallen in love with him again. Probably had never fallen out of it in the first place. And hell, she wanted nothing more than to feel his massive arms around her right now. At least then she'd feel safe. Secure. And not alone. "The only difference is I would've trusted my partner."

Bennett didn't have a chance to answer.

"Over here." Her fingers grazed over a door frame in the darkness. She slid her palm across the freezing metal. Knocking once, she set her ear against the steel. There was nothing on the other side as far as she could tell. Hopefully no one waiting to put a handful of bullets in their chests. Maybe they were going to escape this nightmare after all. She ran her hands along the metal. What kind of door didn't have a doorknob? "Okay, maybe not."

"Let me see." Heavy footsteps approached from behind. Bennett's hands collided with hers as he inspected the door by feel, and she drew back. He launched his shoulder into the steel. Once. Twice.

It wouldn't budge. A rough exhale feathered against her chilled skin and she ran her hands up and down her arms for warmth. If Jamie Mascaro planned on leaving them in here to freeze to death, she had a good start. "Is it still considered a door if there's no way to open it?"

Glennon faced the rest of the space. "There has to be another way out of here. Isn't it against code to only have one exit?"

"Do you honestly believe Mascaro is concerned with the building code?" Bennett's voice shook, whether from the drugs or the dropping temperatures, she didn't know. Either way, they didn't have much time. Jamie Mascaro was going to kill her and Bennett, or else the warehouse would. "I ran with Nicholas and his crew for over a year. I know every property he acquired to store the stolen weapons. This isn't one of them."

"I don't think knowing the property would make any difference against a team of armed infantry-men." Movement from under the lit doorway rocketed her pulse into dangerous territory. A weapon. She patted herself down then rushed toward one of the trucks a few feet away. They needed something to fight off Mascaro and her operatives.

Glennon pulled herself up the single step to the passenger-side door. There. The broken shifter. She wrenched the door open, the hinges screaming in protest. Bringing a metal pipe to a gunfight wasn't the best idea, but it was the only shot they had. She traced a path back to the spot they'd been bound, then to the door.

Bennett took up the other side. Waiting.

The door opened. Yellow light spilled across the floor, outlining two distinct shadows.

Glennon swung as hard as she could. Metal connected with bone, the crunch sickening and loud. The soldier hit the ground as another rushed forward. Bennett collided with the operative, taking him to the ground. Two more surged through the door, both armed with assault rifles, and took aim.

She tossed the pipe and backed away from the door, hands raised in surrender. Fear thickened in her veins. This was it. These men were going to kill her. She'd never get the chance to tell Anthony why she'd left Anchorage in the first place. Never see her son again. Her throat tightened as she fought to breathe evenly. This couldn't be it. Not yet. He deserved to know she loved him.

The echo of heels on cement grew louder. Then stopped. Overhead lighting highlighted Jamie Mascaro's thin lips and stone-cold expression. The skin-tight black leather dress accentuated the woman's curves, but it was the hatred in her expression that raised the hairs on the back of Glennon's neck.

"Bring them with us as collateral." Mascaro closed in, studying Glennon's features from forehead to chin before turning away. "We've got company."

Chapter Fourteen

The Grim Reaper wasn't supposed to fall in love, but that rule had gone out the window a long time ago. Jamie Mascaro could beat him, take his life or break his soul, but he'd be damned if he let her take Glennon.

He crouched along the shoreline of Tina Lake, the MK 17 SCAR assault rifle from his trunk resting across his thighs. Abandoned vehicles, semi-trailers, mountains of dirt and greenery all held potential for an ambush. Too many possibilities. At this time of night, the entire area had been vacated. Perfect for a militarized criminal organization to operate undetected. Gravel—the same color Vincent had matched to their shooter from Helen Chase's home—slid through his fingers easily. No movement. But that didn't mean they weren't alone. Four warehouses, any of which could hold two Military Police investigators.

And time was running out.

"I counted five operatives at the exchange, all

armed with M4s, plus the leader, but I'm not taking any chances." And with his son handed off into Vincent's care after the team had met him on location, he could focus on getting Glennon back. Standing, Anthony brushed dirt off his hand along his pants, his Kevlar vest pressing on his shoulders. He faced off with Elizabeth Dawson and Elliot Dunham, their features and choice of weapons highlighted by construction spotlights surrounding the area.

A former NSA consultant and a con artist. Not soldiers, but just as reliable and just as dangerous under the right circumstances. And these were the right circumstances. "We'll search this first building then move on to the next until we find Jamie Mascaro's hideout. Liz, you're at the north entrance." He pointed straight ahead. "Elliot, at the east. I'll take the south. Your earpieces have GPS if you're taken. Meet back here in five to search the next building. We good?"

He tapped the small earbud in his left ear. Both teammates cringed from the sound.

"Good." Elizabeth unholstered her weapon from beneath her black leather jacket, both hands tight on the grip.

"I'm thinking I should've brought a bigger gun." Elliot raised one hand. "Can I switch with you?"

"How about I ignore your GPS if you're taken? Let's move. Mascaro won't keep our targets alive long." If she hadn't tied up the loose ends already.

No. He couldn't think like that. The second he gave in to that line of thinking, there was no telling what he might do. Or who he might kill. Anthony kept low and moved fast to the south end of the first warehouse, gravel crunching under his boots.

"Do you think he'll really ignore my GPS if I'm kidnapped?" Elliot's whispers died as he and Elizabeth moved around the east side of the building.

Setting one shoulder into the door, Anthony pressed his ear to the steel. Nothing. The breeze rustled the weeds lining the lake a few hundred yards away, a couple red foxes wrestling along the shore. But no sound of movement from behind the door, as far as he could tell.

He tested the lock then hiked the rifle into his shoulder. His instincts screamed in warning. Who left a warehouse like this unlocked in the middle of the night? Maneuvering in front of the entrance, Anthony wrenched the door open and slapped his hand into position on the rifle. The answer came easily enough: a criminal mastermind who expected company.

Darkness consumed him as he heel-toed it into the building. His heart beat steadily in his chest, the rest of his senses on high alert. He didn't need to see in the dark to find Glennon. This was what he'd trained for, what he'd been hired for. This was what he did best. Steel reverberated underneath him as he stepped onto an overhead walkway. He scanned the space below with what little light reached across the warehouse floor. Oil barrels, haul trucks, a couple forklifts. Alaska was known for its oil exports. This place had obviously been one of the six oil refinery storage warehouses in the state.

He moved down the center walkway. His thigh holster ricocheted off one of the handrails, the ping of metal loud in his ears. Anthony tightened his hold on the rifle's grip. So much for the element of surprise.

The walkway sparked as gunfire erupted off to his right.

He hit the walkway hard. The raised metal edges cut into his cheek, but didn't distract from the shooter below. Shoving to his feet, Anthony swung his rifle over the handrail and down toward the shooter. One pull of the trigger. Two. The rifle kicked back into his shoulder. He released the breath he'd been holding. No return fire. Either he'd hit the soldier or the shooter had started searching for a better shot.

Keeping aim, he moved across the walkway, deeper into the warehouse. Adrenaline rushed through his veins. Light from an open door spilled across the cement floor. And there, right at the edge of darkness, was a pair of boots. He tapped his earpiece, moving to the other side of the warehouse. "I've got one down. Report."

"Two down for me," Elizabeth said. "Looks like we're in the right place after all."

"Oh, man. You guys got to shoot people already?" Elliot's heavy breathing crackled over the line. "I've got nothing but offices on this side of the building. And they're all empty so far."

"That makes three. We're missing at least two more, plus Jamie Mascaro." Anthony took the stairs two at a time. Swinging the rifle across the large space, he kicked at the downed operative's boots. He'd been shot all right. Two bullets. One to the soldier's vest, the other to his throat. He wasn't getting up anytime soon. "The warehouse is clear."

"The offices are clear," Elliot said in his ear.

"I'm clear here, too," Elizabeth said. "There's no one else here."

"Mascaro wouldn't have left three men behind for nothing. We're missing something." Anthony searched the rest of the space. Dark spots interrupted the muted gray color of the cement floor about ten feet away. His footsteps echoed off the oil barrels as he followed the pattern to the west side of the building, toward the lake. Could be oil. Could be… He locked onto the wide roll-top door. Blood. He tapped the earpiece. "Oil warehouses like this would need access to the water to load barrels onto ships for distribution." He pulled his shoulders back. "They're on the docks."

Sliding his finger along the trigger, Anthony took a single step toward the door. Something crunched under his boot. Four distinct zip ties littered the floor. Fury burned through him. Two for Glennon and two for Bennett? He kicked them out of the way. They'd been broken. Maybe she and her partner had gotten loose? Didn't explain the blood, but at least that line of thought interrupted the rage threatening to rip him apart from the inside. He took a deep, cleansing breath. Glennon had always been the one to bring him back from the edge when he'd come home from tour, and he prayed like hell she could do it when this was over.

"I want everyone on the west side of the building in thirty seconds."

"Copy that," Elizabeth said. "On my way."

Elliot reported in next. "You got it, man."

He kicked the padlock that secured the roll-top door out of the way, pulling at the chains along the wall, forgoing the element of surprise. A rush of Alaskan air raised the goose bumps at the back of his neck—clean, crisp. With a hint of rose. He held on to that scent with everything he had. Glennon. She was close. He stepped out into the open. "I'm coming, sweetheart."

Pain splintered across the right side of his head. He jerked away from the hit, swinging the rifle toward his assailant. A kick to the chest knocked Anthony to the ground, his head hitting hard, and the gun slid across the asphalt. Vision blurred, he fought to focus. Damn it. Groping for his nearest weapon, Anthony shoved to his feet, blade in hand. One target. He ran full-force, swinging his arm out wide.

His attacker ducked under his arm then came

around and wrapped both arms under his shoulders and around his neck. Pressure built in his chest the longer the soldier cut off his air, grip tight over his trachea. Rookie move. His head pounded in rhythm with his heartbeat, the stitches in his thigh and rib cage protesting, but all it took was one shift in weight and Anthony heaved his assailant into the ground. He slammed his elbow back into the attacker's face. Once. Twice. Blood splattered against his long-sleeved shirt. The rifle was close, but by the time he got to it, the soldier would have the advantage. Not going to happen.

The unsheathing of a blade forced Anthony to roll. Rock and ice cut into him as he returned to his feet. He wrenched backward at a swing of his opponent's blade. Blocking the second swing, he caught the attacker's wrist and nearly snapped the damn thing in two. Metal on asphalt rang in his ears a split second before a scream broke the steady lapping of water nearby.

Hiking the bastard into him, he growled, "Where is she?"

Two spotlights blazed to life over the docks, spilling light across the wide-open expanse of gravel.

"We've been expecting you, Sergeant Major Harris." Jamie Mascaro stood in front of a dumpster centered between two docks, high heels sinking into the dirt. "Time to finish this."

Shoving the heel of his boot into the soldier's knee, he took the fighter out of commission. Another scream penetrated his haze of rage. He released his hold as he turned to face the newest threat. His opponent collapsed. He wasn't even sorry for the lifelong pain and discomfort the man would have to endure.

Elizabeth and Elliot rounded from the east side of the building, weapons up, waiting on his order.

"I couldn't agree more." He took two steps forward. "Give me what I came for and you might make it out of here alive."

"You're not exactly in a position to make demands, Ranger." Jamie Mascaro snapped her fingers. A second set of spotlights flickered, illuminating the last two soldiers positioned at the end of each dock. One guarding Bennett, the other with Glennon. They were alive. Relief spread a burning sensation across Anthony's chest, but not for long. Each was tied to a chair on the end of the separate docks. Gagged, vulnerable, the military investigators fought to get free.

The setup was simple. If he went for one, Mascaro would order the opposite soldier to push the other into the lake. Would let them drown. "Tell me, Anthony, what's more important to you. Love?" Jamie Mascaro swung her arm out, toward Glennon. "Or duty?"

THERE WAS NO WAY Anthony could save them both in time.

Glennon glanced at the soldier watching over her, the one with blood dried across his face from a pipe to the nose. She fought back a smile. The one who'd put his hands on her son. Tasked with making sure she didn't get loose again, he'd zip-tied her wrists behind her back this time, but he'd been in a rush. Enough of a rush that she'd been able to work her knuckles against each other in an attempt to snap the plastic. The flood of relief at seeing Anthony drained her. How could it not? There was no way both she and Bennett would get out of this alive. It was one or the other. Use Bennett to take down Jamie Mascaro and the rest of her operation or save Glennon. And if the teammates he'd recruited as backup interfered? Mascaro was sure to get rid of both her and Bennett simultaneously.

That had been the beauty of her plan.

But… Her gaze cut to the sidearm strapped to her guard's leg. There was more than one way to break a zip tie. Curling her fingers into her palms, she closed her eyes. She hadn't died in that warehouse. She wasn't going to die out here on the dock.

"What's it going to be, Ranger? Use Sergeant Spencer to bring me and my operation to justice or save the woman you love?" Jamie Mascaro wagged her red-tipped index finger from side to side. "Tick-tock, ticktock."

Anthony curled his fingers into a fist. Even from this distance, Glennon noted the hard shift in his expression and her heart pumped a frenzied beat in her chest. Air rushed from her lungs and the gag in her mouth warmed. She recognized that look. Anthony Harris no longer stared out through the dark blue eyes she hadn't been able to get out of her mind the last five years. He'd been replaced by the man who'd had to shoot his way out of Afghanistan to survive, the man who blamed himself for his team's deaths.

The man who'd slowly taken pieces of the Ranger she'd loved every time he'd come home from tour. She couldn't lose another piece of him. She wouldn't.

"Who said anything about justice?" Anthony fanned his grip over his firearm.

A shiver chased down her spine, the chair protesting with the slight shake of her body. But the creak of wood wasn't enough to draw her guard's attention. She needed something more—anything—before it was too late.

"Time's up." Jamie Mascaro angled her head over her shoulder. Toward Glennon.

Planting her knuckles against each other, Glennon forced them together with everything she had. Pain bolted into her wrists and forearms, but she ignored it. The zip tie snapped and she reached for the soldier's sidearm. She wrapped her fingers around the grip but wasn't fast enough.

A rough hand clamped on top of hers a split second before agony exploded across the right side of her head. She hit the dock hard, splinters working their way under her fingers. A predatory growl ripped through the haze closing in on her. Her vision blurred. Gunfire echoed off the lake. The operative fisted a chunk of her hair, wrenching Glennon to her feet. She grabbed at his hand to relieve the spread of pain, her jaw locked against the groan working up her throat.

A bullet clipped her attacker's shoulder and he spun fast, taking her to the ground with him.

A splash of water reached her ears.

Dread sank like a stone in her stomach. Bennett. The soldier assigned to guard him had pushed him into the water and had started firing on Anthony and his team. She rammed the heel of her hand into her guard's bullet wound as hard as she could, but the grip in her hair refused to let up. Raising her hands, she slammed her forearms into his. His hold dropped and she ducked as the soldier reached to secure her again. She planted her hands against his chest and shoved him only mere inches. She went for the gun in his thigh holster again, barely unholstering the Glock before he kicked it out of her hand. It hit the dock, out of reach. She dove for the weapon as two more gunshots cut through the silence from the other dock. Her fingertips skimmed the metal as her guard pulled her back to him by her boot.

"Elliot, no!" Elizabeth Dawson's warning pierced through the gunfire.

"I'm hit!" Elliot said.

Oh, no. One of Anthony's team had been taken down. The soldier flipped her onto her back, pinning her beneath him. They had to get to Bennett. Without him, Jamie Mascaro's operation would live. Millions more military weapons would reach the country's enemies.

Long fingers wrapped around her throat. She tried prying her guard's grip loose. But he was too strong. Too heavy. She kicked against him, but he wouldn't let up. Darkness closed in. Pressure built in her chest—there was no way for her to get the oxygen out. Glennon bucked again.

Wrenching her off the dock, the soldier slammed her head back against the old wood.

Her body wouldn't respond to her brain's commands. Get up. She had to get up. Stars in the night sky blurred, her attacker's face losing definition. Ringing filled her ears.

Low, fast-paced vibrations reverberated along the dock. A gun barrel slid into her vision, aimed between the operative's eyes. Then *he* slid into her vision. Her heart stopped. Stopped then started racing. The man staring out through those dark blue eyes was blood and death and war, but in that moment he was everything she needed him to be. "I've been looking for you."

The operative released her, raising his hands over his head as he stood.

She swallowed against the bruising tightness in her throat. Rolling onto her side, Glennon clawed out from under her attacker and coughed to restart her lungs. Her vision cleared, her throat raw. She wrapped her hand around the Glock she'd taken from the soldier and disengaged the safety. Hiking the gun over her shoulder, she used Anthony for balance and climbed to her feet.

"You put your hands on my son," Anthony said over Elizabeth and Elliot's gunshots on the other dock.

The operative's attention slid to Anthony then back to her. "Better hope your bodyguard is a good shot. One bullet isn't going to stop me from carrying out my orders, sweetheart."

"She's not your sweetheart." Anthony fired. Once. Twice. The man assigned to toss her into the lake collapsed. One bullet to the cheek. One to the head. "She's mine."

Exhaustion pulled at her muscles, but it wasn't over yet. Bennett. They had to get to Bennett. A wave of dizziness messed with her balance and she overcorrected. Strong hands righted her. Glennon adjusted her grip on the gun. Her breath heaved in and out of her lungs. She blinked to clear her head. Movement from across the lake drew her attention to the second dock, where Bennett had gone into the water.

Elizabeth and Elliot worked together and hauled her unconscious partner from the depths.

Relief flooded through her. "We've got him—"

A bullet to the shoulder twisted Anthony around, two more sinking home in his thigh and hip as he raised his Beretta. His boot slipped at the edge of the dock and he plunged backward into the lake.

"No!" The water consumed him, beads spraying across her face. Glennon lunged as rough hands wrenched her backward. She gripped her attacker's wrist and hiked it around and up, flattening out the last soldier's arm. One hit with her elbow broke the bone and she used the space between her index finger and thumb to jam his trachea.

He clamped a hand over his throat and hit the dock hard, his wrist still in her grasp.

A gunshot from behind spun Glennon around, fists up.

"You've surprised me, Sergeant Chase. But now, it's just you and me." Jamie Mascaro's heels thudded across the dock. Motioning the injured soldier up with her Ruger, the weapons dealer nodded at Glennon's discarded Glock. He collected it then pushed Glennon forward. One shot. That was all it would take for Jamie Mascaro to get away with kidnapping and murder, to disappear to some non-extradition country while pocketing millions of dollars in profit from the stolen weapons. "You had your suspect. I served my husband up on a silver platter. You arrested Nicholas, but you couldn't let me have this, could you? Couldn't let me show that bastard I wasn't something he owned, that I was strong enough without him."

The gun wobbled in Jamie Mascaro's hand, the

lines around the woman's mouth deeper than Glennon remembered.

"It's over, Mascaro. Sergeant Spencer has all the evidence we need to court-martial the soldiers you recruited, and send you to prison for the rest of your life." The ache in her chest refused to dissipate. It grew stronger every second Anthony stayed beneath the surface. Every second she didn't know whether he'd survived. "There've been too many lives taken already. This doesn't have to end with more blood."

"You took everything from me!" Jamie Mascaro gripped both hands around the Ruger's grip. "And now you're going to pay."

Water splashed from the surface of the lake and the soldier positioned behind Glennon disappeared.

A growl ripped from Anthony's throat, streams of water running down his face. The veins in his arms struggled from beneath his skin as blood dripped to the dock. "Not if I have anything to say about that."

"It's not possible." Jamie Mascaro backed up a step. Her bottom lip quivered as she aimed the Ruger at the Ranger. "Why won't you just die?"

"Anthony!" Glennon shoved him out of the way and lunged. Wrapping her arms around Mascaro, she wrenched the woman to one side, but the edge of the dock was much closer than she'd originally estimated. The world tilted on its axis as they fell into the lake. Water worked into her mouth and nose, freezing her from the inside. Pressure built in her lungs, but she refused to release her grip.

Jamie Mascaro fought, clawing toward the surface, kicking at her with those ridiculous heels. No. She didn't get to take Anthony from her. Glennon tightened her hand around a bare ankle. Mascaro kicked at her again. Shadows passed above them, highlighted by the spotlights. Ten seconds. That was all she needed. Jamie Mascaro would pass out and they could end this nightmare. Her heart pounded hard in her chest. Bubbles escaped her nose and mouth.

A wave of disturbed water rushed against her.

She was running out of air. Her grip on Mascaro's ankle began to slip as darkness closed in.

Chapter Fifteen

He had her.

Anthony tightened his hold on the dripping wet woman in his arms. The horrible clawing in his chest had finally subsided. She'd come too close to death. He'd nearly lost her, but he'd be damn certain he never would again.

Perched at the back of the ambulance, they had a clear view of the scene. He set his chin on the crown of Glennon's head as the EMT ripped the blood pressure cuff from her arm. Her hair had frozen in long, stringy strands, her skin was paler than normal, the hollowness in her features deeper, but Glennon had never been more beautiful to him than in that moment. She'd survived. "Are you in pain?"

"Every inch of me aches." She watched as Jamie Mascaro was led to the back of a police cruiser, a faint smile curling one corner of her mouth. "But I guess that means I'm alive, doesn't it?"

He didn't return her smile. Her partner had been

recovered. Mascaro's operation had been destroyed. Their jobs were done. But every cell in his body raged. "You shouldn't have risked your life like that."

"After everything we've been through, I wasn't about to let that woman put a bullet in you." Her shoulders rose on a strong inhale, her gaze distant. In an instant she focused on him. "Isn't that what love is? Wanting to keep the person you love most in this world safe? It's a choice. And I choose to love you, Ranger. Forever."

A growl vibrated up his throat as he stared down at her. "Say that again."

"What?" she asked. "That I love you?"

"Yes." Heat counteracted the ice working through his veins. "Say it again."

Her eyes brightened, as though she knew exactly what kind of power she held over him. "All right, but on one condition."

"Anything." Whatever she wanted, he'd give it to her. Right now. Right then. Forever. "Anything you need or want from me, it's yours."

"It's time to let it go. That guilt you carry." The light in her expression dimmed. She framed his face with one hand, her fingers driving through his beard. Glennon scanned his features. "I see it in your eyes every time I'm in danger. I see it in the way you don't hesitate to pull that trigger. Or in the way you put your life at risk time and again to protect me. You believe you could've done more for your team on tour, but I'm here to tell you, you couldn't have saved them. You did everything you could and I'm proud of you."

How could she possibly know that? Heat climbed up his spine. Anthony dropped his arm from around her, flashes of that battle to survive fresh in his mind. But Glennon fisted her fingers around his soaked Kevlar vest to keep him from retreating. She pulled him close, grounding him, keeping him in the moment.

"Glennon—"

"You're scared to lose anyone else. I've understood that more in the last three days than you'll ever know, but you're not the man I fell in love with when that guilt turns you into the Grim Reaper. You're not mine and you can't be a father with it hanging over your head." Dropping her hold, Glennon started to back away, and his pulse rocketed into his throat. "You have a new team—" she nodded toward Elliot and Elizabeth stitching up their wounds "—and now you have a family. We need *you*. Here. Now. Not a ghost of you."

Anthony engulfed her hands in his, studying the small freckles across the backs. He'd lived on that guilt, pushed himself harder, survived. Now he was supposed to let it go? How? "Is that why you left? Why you kept my son from me?"

Remnants of fury coated his words. How could he forgive her for that?

Running her thumb over the patch on his vest with one hand, she notched his chin higher with the other. "Every time you came home, you were different—lost—and I didn't understand. I didn't know what to do or how to help you. And after the last time…I left.

"I was pregnant and scared. I didn't know how much of you would come home or if you'd stay after I told you. But I was wrong." Glennon sniffled, crystalized beads of water sticking to her eyelashes. "I'm sorry. I'm sorry we wasted so much time, that I lied to you—"

Anthony pulled her into him, crushing his mouth down on hers. Because he had to. Because not kissing her had been eating at him since he'd pulled her out of that water. His fingers tangled in the frozen hair at the back of her neck as a groan escaped up his throat. A shiver rocked through her. From the desperation in his hold on her or from the dropping temperatures, he didn't know. Either way, he'd never let go of her again. And he'd be the man she needed. He'd do whatever it took. If that meant taking himself out of the protection game or going to support meetings, he'd do it. For her. For Hunter. For their family.

Anthony pulled away first.

"I want you more than any job, more than the breath in my lungs and more than anything else in this world. I'm here, sweetheart. One hundred percent." He set his forehead against hers but kept her close, pressed into him. Her rose scent, buried under a layer of lake smells, worked down into his lungs. "You never have to worry about that side of me again. He's gone. And I'm not going anywhere."

"Good. Neither am I." Wrapping long fingers around his wrists, she closed her eyes and huddled deeper into the blanket the EMT had wrapped around her, a puddle pooling at her feet. Excess water from the lake seeped into his own clothing, freezing him to the core, but Anthony wasn't going anywhere. Not without her. "I need to get out of these clothes."

"I can help with that." He bent his mouth to hers, savoring her for another few short seconds before reality set in. Reports. Following up with Anchorage PD. Filling in the army. Reporting to Sullivan for his next assignment.

"First, take me to our son," she said, "then you can take us home."

"To the cabin?" Even on the verge of hypothermia, Glennon Chase was determined to put their son first. And he loved her for it.

He stood, with effort. Threading his fingers through hers, Anthony pulled her to him. Desire raked down his spine at her touch as he fit her against him. Right where she belonged. A quick nod solidified his plans for the future. Her and Hunter. His family. Everything he'd ever wanted. A smile curled his mouth as he planted a quick kiss to her lips. "Absolutely, sweetheart."

Red-and-blue lights illuminated the scene. The

coroner's van was parked at the far end of the parking lot. Anchorage PD would want a full report, but that could wait. Glennon was his priority. She was all that mattered.

Medics wheeled Bennett Spencer past them to a second ambulance. Hypothermia. A bullet in the shoulder, another in the rib cage. He'd live. The bastard was too stubborn to die.

"Hey, hold up," Anthony called to the EMTs, motioning to the gurney with his chin. They slowed. An oxygen mask blocked most of Bennett's face. The guy looked like he'd been to hell and back. Barely conscious, blood staining his shirt, eyes sagging closed. But this couldn't wait. "Glennon wouldn't be here if it wasn't for you. I owe you."

Bennett blinked slowly at him, every breath a rasp. "Is…th-that appreciation I…h-hear?"

"Don't flatter yourself." Glancing down at Glennon, he tightened his hold on the only woman who'd been able to break him. If it hadn't been for Bennett, he wouldn't be standing there. And Glennon… He'd have lost her all over again. He'd have lost everything. "I know a good JAG Corp prosecutor. Call the office and ask for Jane Reise. Tell her I sent you. Then, when you're clear of all the charges the army will level against you, come work for us. Blackhawk Security could use an operative like you."

Laugh lines deepened around Bennett's eyes. "Tall, dark…and hand…some?"

A laugh burst from between Glennon's pale lips.

"I take it back. You're obviously delusional from loss of blood." Squeezing her into his side, Anthony nodded at the EMTs on either side of the gurney. "Get him out of here before I change my mind."

The gurney bounced over uneven ground before the EMTs loaded Bennett into the back of the ambulance.

Steering Glennon toward his waiting SUV, Anthony studied the scene one last time. The investigation was over. Jamie Mascaro would serve the rest of her life behind bars in a women's correctional facility, within a stone's throw of the husband she'd betrayed. Glennon could put in for discharge and they could finally start their lives together. But not until—

"Mommy!" Hunter's excited voice carried over the noise of one ambulance siren and the ongoing conversations between officers. The four-year-old rushed across the gravel, leaving Vincent in the slush. Three seconds. That was all it took him to reach his mother.

Dropping to her knees, Glennon wrapped him in an all-consuming hug, planting her face into the space between his neck and shoulder. Her fingers moved along his back and dug into his shoulders. Nothing in the world would be able to part them, and Anthony would kill anyone who tried. "I missed you. Are you okay?"

Hunter nodded as the Blackhawk Security's forensics expert trod across the scene. The crooked smile Anthony couldn't get out of his mind flashed wide. "Vincent showed me how to dial 9-1-1!"

"Yeah, you were supposed to leave that part out." A big smile, surrounded by a full beard, creased the laugh lines around Vincent Kalani's brown eyes, and something significant shifted. The ex-cop never smiled. He was too serious. Too hell-bent on revenge. In the year or so Anthony had known the forensics expert, he'd never seen those pearly whites. Seemed Hunter had that effect on a lot of people.

"How very thoughtful." Glennon lightened her hold on her son long enough to throw an amused glance in Anthony's direction, and he couldn't help but laugh. "Laugh all you want, Ranger. You're going to be the one to wake up when Anchorage PD shows up at our door at three in the morning."

His laugh died as he narrowed his gaze on Vincent. "You're a dead man."

Something—no, someone—tugged on the bottom of his T-shirt. Hunter stared up at him, green eyes bright. He pulled Anthony to his knees and reached into his jacket pocket. Cupping his hand alongside his mouth, he looked over his shoulder toward his mother. The boy kept his voice low, but not low enough that Glennon couldn't hear. "Can we give Mommy her present now?"

With a single nod and a faint salute, Vincent backed toward his waiting SUV.

"Sure, buddy." Anthony held out his hand, careful to hide the gift from prying eyes. "Do you want to help?"

An enthusiastic nod curled Hunter's mouth into a smile. Anthony moved his son into position beside him. "Okay. Come here."

"When did you guys have time to get me a present?" Standing, Glennon cut her gaze to Hunter, a smile overwhelming the paleness in her features. Confusion deepened the three distinct lines between her eyebrows.

"Down on one knee, buddy." Curling one arm around their son, Anthony mimicked Hunter's position, groaning through the new stitches in his thigh, then raised his focus to Glennon. Every muscle in his body caught fire at the sight of her. This was it. Now or never. He lowered his mouth to his son's ear. "Here we go. Say, 'Sergeant Glennon Chase.'"

"Sergeant Glennon Chase." Hunter's small voice grew louder with each word.

"What's going on?" Glennon dropped her hands to her sides, shifting her weight between both feet. Her attention ping-ponged between him and her son. "What are you doing?"

"We love you with all our heart." Anthony waited as the boy repeated every word, anticipation spreading through his chest. Every officer, Blackhawk Security operative and even the medicolegal investigator watched in silence. "We want you to be ours forever."

"We want you to be ours forever." Hunter spun from side to side, clasping his hands.

Anthony focused on the woman he'd never fallen out of love with—this beautiful, intelligent, caring, badass woman of his—offering her the gift in his hand. Slush worked through his pants as he tightened his hold around Hunter, but he didn't give a damn. He'd kneel here all night if it meant spending forever with her. With the chain looped around his middle finger, he let go. Flickering patrol lights reflected off her engagement ring as it twisted at the end of the chain. "So will you make us a family?"

One month later...

DAWN BROKE OVER the Chugach Mountain range. Perfect and cleansing.

Glennon reached out, a line of tears burning in her lower lash line as she squeezed her mother's hand. She blinked the moisture back. Her engagement band spun around the oversensitized skin of her ring finger. She couldn't breathe. Couldn't think. Was this really happening? The two most important people in the world waited for her near Campbell Lake's shoreline, but all she could do was stand there.

"Are you ready?" Helen asked.

"Hell yes." With both Mascaros behind bars, she'd

submitted her discharge papers and left the army behind. She'd sold her house and moved her and her son across the country to a city she'd been determined never to step foot in again. All to be with Anthony. This was just the next step in that plan. She couldn't wait to start a life with her weapons expert. Everything she'd ever wanted waited down the aisle lined with dozens of pinecones from the nearby tree line. Her future. Her family.

The entire Blackhawk Security team rose as she got into position. Everyone except Bennett, who she wouldn't see for twelve to eighteen months after his sentencing. She raised her toes to hit the inside top of her black rain boots. "I'm ready."

Music reached her ears as she and her mother passed a stack of fresh firewood lined with white candles. Tightening her hand around the collection of wildflowers, she set sights on the man she planned to spend the rest of her life with.

Four days of stolen moments. Four days of near-death experiences. Four days of rediscovering why she'd fallen in love with Anthony Harris in the first place. That was all it had taken. Her fear of losing him to his overachieving sense of duty had vanished the second he'd dove into the lake to save her rather than take down Jamie Mascaro. The rules had gone out the window then. Hell, they might've gone out the window the moment she'd dialed his number for help. They seemed so…worthless now.

He was a protector, and a damn good one at that. He'd done his job while she'd barely held things together. And wasn't that what she needed most in the man she wanted to raise her child with? Someone she could rely on, trust? Someone who would protect her and their son with every fiber of his being?

Glennon sucked in a deep breath. She'd never had a chance when it came to him. He was hers from the minute he'd walked in to teach her firearms class in basic training all those years ago. And she'd always been his.

She studied Hunter, his expression full of anticipation. Her lips spread into a smile. Dressed in a black suit and shirt with a bright red tie, the exact same color as his father's, her son held on to Anthony with everything he had. Her Ranger—their protector—held on just as tight.

Gravel crunched under her boots as she headed down the aisle, Helen at her side. Sullivan, his significant other, Jane, Elizabeth, Vincent, Kate, even Elliot in his sling smiled and nodded as she passed. She fought to keep time with the music, but impatience tightened her fingers around the bouquet of wildflowers. The shoot-out with Jamie Mascaro hadn't taken this long. She rolled her numb lips between her teeth. This was it. This was what forever felt like.

Getting married in the middle of January had seemed ridiculous when Anthony had suggested it. But now? Glennon couldn't wait another second without being married to her man.

"Pick up the pace, Mom." Tugging Helen along with her, she closed the distance between her and Anthony, the quartet scrambling to keep up with the change in pace. Laughter echoed off the pines surrounding them, but she pushed it to the back of her mind.

A wide smile flashed across Anthony's features, his beard speckled with fresh snowflakes.

"Here we go." Spinning into her mother, she kissed each side of Helen's face. "Thanks, Mom. For protecting me. For giving me a safe haven." She clasped both hands in hers. "For teaching me how to shoot a gun." A laugh broke through the sudden burst of emotion bubbling to the surface. "And for being there for me when I needed you the most."

"Come on, girl, I ain't dying. Not until I see my daughter married anyway." A single tear raced down Helen's wrinkled cheek. She wiped a strand of hair out of Glennon's face. "But I will say one thing. I'm proud of you, baby girl. You turned out exactly as I hoped, and I'm gonna take full credit for that." Laughter filled the clearing again as Helen turned her attention to Anthony. "And you. Don't make me use my shotgun on you, you hear?"

"Yes, ma'am." Anthony clasped his hands in front of him and nodded. Laughter glittered in his eyes and Glennon's heart skipped a beat. Even after all these years, he affected her in new ways every second she laid eyes on him. "You have my word."

Helen took her seat, leaving Glennon with her Ranger. Sliding his calloused hands into hers, he helped maneuver her opposite him. Blue eyes, the same color as the sky above them, settled on her, and the world faded. Everything—the flickering candles off to her right, the temperature—disappeared. Only she, Hunter and Anthony remained.

"We gather here today to finally unite Glennon and Anthony in holy matrimony. And what a journey it's been, from what I understand." The minister's words died on the slight Alaskan breeze coiling through the trees as she studied the man across from her. What seemed like mere seconds later, the priest turned to her weapons expert. "Do you, Anthony, take Glennon as your lawfully wedded wife, in sickness and in health, until death do you part?"

"Before I answer, there are a few things I need to say. But not to you, sweetheart. At least, not yet."

Anthony squeezed her hand then quickly let her go. Suspicion rose the hairs on the back of her neck as he twisted to his left and knelt beside their son. "Hunter, I promise to protect you with my life. I promise to take you fishing even though I don't know how to fish, to tell you funny jokes, to help you with your homework, to give you tips on girls when you're eighteen and I can't stop you from dating, and to watch any show you want to watch, however many times."

Glennon couldn't stop the laugh rising up her throat. He was going to regret that last promise as soon as Hunter got home and forced him to watch every episode of *Mickey Mouse Clubhouse*. Her heart threatened to burst.

"You deserve a dad who can always be there for you, the best dad you could ever ask for." Anthony braced his hands on Hunter's shoulders. "And I'm going to be that guy for you, okay?"

Hunter nodded, biting his bottom lip with all his small upper teeth. Wait. She narrowed her gaze. Was that chocolate around his mouth?

"Do I have your permission to marry your mom now?" he asked.

"Yeah." Hunter crumpled his tie in one hand and gave his father a high-five with the other.

"Thanks, buddy." A single kiss to their son's forehead sealed the deal. This was the man she wanted to spend the rest of her life with.

Anthony straightened, taking her hands in his. "Okay. We're good to go."

The minister started over. "Do you, Anthony, take Glennon as your lawfully wedded wife, in sickness and in health, until death do you part?"

"Not yet," Anthony said. "I have two conditions."

Her shoulders sank. He had to be kidding.

"Let me get this straight. You want me to marry you, but you're negotiating conditions in the middle of our wedding." She forced the tension to drain from

her muscles, but even in the middle of the most perfect day, the day she'd been looking forward to for
over a month, he was determined to make that impossible. "Don't you think this discussion should've
happened *before* the actual wedding?"

"Where's the fun in that?" Anthony winked.
"Glennon, I will never choose any job or anyone, except our son, over you ever again. You are my priority. You are my future. I will never do anything to put
that at risk, and I will do anything to keep you safe.
The first condition I'm setting is that we're honest
with each other for the rest of our lives. No secrets.
And you'll tell me you're pregnant the next time."

She swallowed at the tightening in her throat as
he winked. In vain. A smile pulled at her mouth as
she adjusted her hands in his. He wanted more ba-
bies with her. "Okay. Second condition?"

His quick glance at Hunter raised the hairs on the
back of her neck. With a single nod, her son—*their*
son—coaxed Anthony to go on. What were these
two up to? "Second condition. You need to come
work for Blackhawk Security. As one of our lead
investigators."

"What?" Shock exploded through her. Her mouth
dropped open. The entire reason she'd decided to
quit the army was to spend more time with her son.
Working for Blackhawk Security, starting a brand-
new career… None of that would let her make up for
the long nights and missed weekends. For four years,

she'd relied on someone else showing up at his bedside when the nightmares came, making his favorite breakfast in the morning, taking him to the zoo
when one of her and Bennett's cases got too intense.
Hunter deserved a parent at home, one who could
be there for him to kiss the scratches and scrapes.

Anthony didn't get to take that away from her.
Didn't matter that they were having this conversation in front of the entire Blackhawk Security team.

"Your timing sucks, Ranger." Glennon lowered
her voice, too many prying ears waiting for her answer. "I told you why I was resigning from the army.
Hunter deserves—"

"A parent at home. I know," Anthony said. "Which
is why I told Sullivan a few minutes before the cere-
mony that I will only be taking assignments when
you're home to be with our son."

The air rushed from her lungs. What?

"I know for a fact you love your job, Glennon,
and you're damn good at it." Rough fingers wrapped
around her wrist then slid across the back of her
hand. His body heat battled with the ice setting up
residence under her skin as he took her hand in both
of his. Goose bumps pimpled down her arms as he
studied her, jaw slack, lips parted. "I've seen the way
you work, the way you care about the victims in your
cases. And I never want you to have to give that up.
Not when you can help so many more people."

Truth resonated through her. She loved her job,

everything about it. And he was right. She was damn good at it. But she loved Hunter more. She slid her hand over her son's small chest, pressing his spine into her leg. His heart beat steadily under her palm as Anthony's hand warmed her to the bone. "I don't know what to say."

"Say yes, Glennon," Anthony said. "Then I'll marry you."

Blood rushed from her head. She shifted to keep her balance, her black rain boots squishing along the shoreline. Too much. This was all too much. And he...he was willing to sacrifice his career so she could keep hers. How the hell had she gotten so lucky? She scanned the faces in the audience. "You don't have to do this. I don't need my job. I have savings. I have—"

"I told you I would do anything to make you happy." Diving into his pocket, Anthony extracted a second band, this one embedded with diamonds. "And I meant every word."

Her hand shook as he slid the wedding band onto her finger. She ignored the rush of excitement radiating from the center of her core. She wouldn't have to give up her career. Because of him. A smile consumed the seemingly permanent darkness in his features, and her heart rocketed into her throat. "All right. Then, yes."

"Then it's a deal." He wrapped his hands in hers. Addressing the minister, he kept his attention locked on her. As though she were the only woman in the entire world. "Good to go."

"All right then." The minister leaned in. "Do you, Anthony, take Glennon as your lawfully wedded wife, in sickness and in health, until death do you part?"

"Hell yes, I do," he said.

The minister turned to her. "And do you, Glennon, take Anthony as your lawfully wedded husband, in sickness and in health, until death do you part?"

"Hell yes, I do." Forget the dropping temperatures. With the way her Ranger looked at her now, her blood had started boiling. If he kept this up, she wouldn't need her fur-lined coat during the reception.

"Then I now pronounce you husband and wife," the minister said.

Hollers and clapping echoed off the surrounding trees, but Glennon only had attention for her husband and son. Her heart started beating again.

Hunter clapped along with the guests, jumping up and down.

"And you said you'd never get involved with one of your partners." Anthony kissed her then. The deep, desperate kind of kiss she'd been craving. The kind that told her he'd never choose his job over her or their son, that she was alive because of him and that fear wouldn't stop them from being happy. Never again. "Any other rules I need to know about?"

"Yeah." She shivered as his beard tickled against her lips. "Don't give my mother a reason to shoot you."

* * * * *

I N T R I G U E

Available February 19, 2019

#1839 HOSTAGE AT HAWK'S LANDING
Badge of Justice • by Rita Herron
Dexter Hawk's search for the truth about his father's death leads him to a
homeless shelter where Melissa Gentry, the love of his life, works. Together,
can they stop a dangerous conspiracy that has caused the disappearance of
several transients in the area?

#1840 THE DARK WOODS
A Winchester, Tennessee Thriller • by Debra Webb
Sasha Lenoir has always wondered what happened on the night her parents
died. Now she'll do anything to learn the truth, even if that means employing
the help of US Marshal Branch Holloway—the father of the child she's kept
secret for more than a dozen years.

#1841 TRUSTING THE SHERIFF
by Janice Kay Johnson
Detective Abby Baker can't remember anything from the past week. She
just knows that someone tried to kill her. Placed under Sheriff Caleb Tanner's
protection, can Abby recall what happened before her attacker strikes again?

#1842 STORM WARNING
by Michele Hauf
When a woman is killed, police chief Jason Cash wonders if the killer
attacked the wrong person, since Yvette LaSalle, a mysterious foreigner with
the same first name as the victim, seems to be hiding in the remote town.
Can Jason protect Yvette from an unknown enemy?

#1843 UNDERCOVER PREGNANCY
by Alice Sharpe
Following a helicopter crash, Chelsea Pierce remembers nothing—not even
the fact that Adam Parish, the man who saved her, is the father of her unborn
child. With determined killers closing in, will Adam and Chelsea be able to
save themselves...and their baby?

#1844 THE GIRL WHO COULDN'T FORGET
by Cassie Miles
Twelve years ago, Brooke Josephson and five other girls were kidnapped.
Now Brooke and FBI special agent Justin Sloan must discover why Brooke's
friend, another former captive, was murdered. Could the psychopath from
her childhood be back and ready to finish what he started?

**YOU CAN FIND MORE INFORMATION ON UPCOMING HARLEQUIN® TITLES,
FREE EXCERPTS AND MORE AT WWW.HARLEQUIN.COM.**

HICNM0219

Get 4 FREE REWARDS!

We'll send you 2 FREE Books plus 2 FREE Mystery Gifts.

Harlequin Intrigue® books feature heroes and heroines that confront and survive danger while finding themselves irresistibly drawn to one another.

FREE
Value Over
$20

He knew she was shaken, but he wasn't ready to let her out of his
sight. "Melissa, you could have been hurt tonight." Killed, but
he couldn't allow himself to voice that awful thought aloud. "I'll
see that you get home safely, so don't argue."

Melissa rubbed a hand over her eyes. She was obviously so
exhausted she simply nodded and slipped from his SUV. Just as
he thought, the beat-up minivan belonged to her.

She jammed her key in the ignition, the engine taking three
tries to sputter to life.

Anger that she sacrificed so much for others mingled with
worry that she might have died doing just that.

She deserved so much better. To have diamonds and pearls.
At least a car that didn't look as if it had been rolled twice.

He glanced back at the shelter before he pulled from the
parking lot. Melissa was no doubt worried about the men she'd
had to move tonight. But worry for her raged through him.

He knew good and damn well that many of the men who
ended up in shelters had simply fallen on hard times and needed a
hand. But others…the drug addicts, mentally ill and criminals…

He didn't like the fact that Melissa put herself in danger by
trying to help them. Tonight's incident proved the facility wasn't
secure.

The thought of losing her bothered him more than he wanted
to admit as he followed her through the streets of Austin. His gut
tightened when she veered into an area consisting of transitional
homes. A couple had been remodeled, but most looked as if they

were teardowns. The street was not in the best part of town, either, and was known for shady activities, including drug rings and gangs.

Her house was a tiny bungalow with a sagging little porch and paint-chipped shutters, and sat next to a rotting shanty, where two guys in hoodies hovered by the side porch, heads bent in hushed conversation as if they might be in the middle of a drug deal.

He gritted his teeth as he parked and walked up the graveled path to the front porch. She paused, her key in hand. A handcrafted wreath said Welcome Home, which for some reason twisted his gut even more.

Melissa had never had a real home, while he'd grown up on the ranch with family and brothers and open land.

She offered him a small smile. "Thanks for following me, Dex."

"I'll go in and check the house," he said, itching to make sure that at least her windows and doors were secure. From his vantage point now, it looked as if a stiff wind would blow the house down.

She shook her head. "That's not necessary, but I appreciate it." She ran a shaky hand through her hair. "I'm exhausted. I'm going to bed."

She opened the door and ducked inside without another word and without looking back. An image of her crawling into bed in that lonely old house taunted him.

He wanted to join her. Hold her. Make sure she was all right tonight.

But that would be risky for him.

Still, he couldn't shake the feeling that she was in danger as he walked back to his SUV.

Don't miss
Hostage at Hawk's Landing *by Rita Herron,*
available March 2019 wherever
Harlequin® Intrigue books and ebooks are sold.

www.Harlequin.com

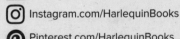